Texas Double Date

Port Serenity Series

Ann DeFee

BELLASTORIA PRESS
Books that nurture the soul

Holt Medallion Award of Merit

ISBN 978-1-942209-30-0

Cover design by WickedSmartDesign.com

Bellastoria Press
P.O. Box 60341
Longmeadow, MA 01116
info@bellastoriapress.com
www.bellastoriapress.com

Prologue

"Come give your mama some sugar."

Sunny McAllister flew into her mom's arms. Mama's lovin' was better than a hot fudge sundae, better than a Barbie doll at Christmas, better than anything Sunny could imagine. She stretched her arms out as far as they'd go. "I love you bigger than the whole wide world."

Renata and Sunny were a two member team. They didn't have a coach. They didn't have a cheering section. They didn't even have a daddy. Sunny would sometimes see a big family on the beach and wonder what it would be like to have a grandma and a couple of cousins. But that probably wasn't going to happen, so Mama was everything in her little universe.

"You're the sunshine of my life," Mama said as Sunny snuggled in her lap.

They'd been playing this game as long as Sunny could remember, but something seemed different tonight. She was tempted to put her thumb in her mouth, but kindergarteners didn't do stuff like that. "I wish you didn't have to work."

"I know, baby. But sometimes we have to do things we don't want to. Like when you have to help me pull weeds."

"I hate weeds," Sunny said, adding a frown.

"Me, too." Mama gave her a high-five. "Tomorrow we'll go to the beach and have ice cream. How does that sound?"

"Can I have chocolate with lots of sprinkles?"

"Absolutely." Mama kissed the top of her

daughter's head. "I've got to get going. Mrs. Burke said she'll be here in five minutes. I hate leaving you, but Joe at the café has been slammed by a busload of tourists. Lock the door and don't let anyone in but Mrs. Burke."

Sunny knew all the rules. Don't talk to strangers. Be polite to grown-ups. Say her prayers at night. And don't open the door to anyone but her babysitter. "Yes. ma'am."

"It's a frog stranger out there." Mama grabbed her raincoat. "I'm going to be soaked by the time I get to the diner." Renata shrugged and then gave Sunny another kiss. "You'll be in dreamland by the time I get back. Be a good girl," she said before walking off into the rainy night.

Sunny was learning to tell time so she watched the clock waiting for Mrs. Burke—fifteen minutes had passed, then twenty. Had something bad happened to her babysitter?

All of a sudden red and blue lights were bouncing off the walls of the trailer—flashing around and around like the lights in the disco movie. Sunny peeked through the blinds and saw a police car in front of Mrs. Burke's trailer.

Sunny was so scared she thought she might pee her panties. She didn't want anyone to know she was home alone, so she turned off the lights and watched thru the blinds. The thought of staying by herself made her tummy ache. She thought going outside to find a policeman, but then an ambulance pulled up and a couple of men in uniforms jumped out and ran inside Mrs. Burke's trailer. Something really, really horrible was going on. What would Mama want her to do? Sunny was trying really not to cry so she snuggled down on the couch and pulled the afghan over her head. If she stayed very, very still, maybe she'd be safe. And if she went to sleep, Mama would be home when she woke up.

Mama always told her to sing when she couldn't go to sleep. That must have worked because the next thing Sunny knew someone was pounding on the front door. The rain was hitting the outside of the trailer, but the lights from the police cars were gone. Why would someone be pounding on the door?

"Please God, please God make the bad man go away. Please, please, please." Sunny whispered over and over until the pounding stopped. She cried herself to sleep, hoping, praying that Mama would be home in the morning. But when she woke up the trailer was silent and Mama still wasn't home. Her stomach hurt and the inside of her head felt as if it had been stuffed with cotton balls. Where was mama? She'd tried calling the diner but the phone rang and rang, and no one answered.

Sunny poured a bowl of Captain Crunch that tasted like cardboard and then ran next door to Mrs. Burke's trailer. She banged and banged on the door but no one answered. School was her only safe place, so she dressed and trudged to the bus stop. What if Mama never came home?

Sunny adored school. She loved reading, and learning and she was crazy about Mrs. Hamilton, her teacher. Plus, she had lots of friends to play with at recess. But today a dark cloud surrounded her, making her want to cry and hide so the bad things wouldn't get her. She couldn't go back to that dark trailer. She was tired, and hungry, and just the thought of going back to that empty house scared her witless.

"Ms. Hamilton, may I talk to you?" She'd finally gotten up the courage to tell her

Mrs. Hamilton looked like a princess with golden hair and pretty blue eyes.

"Sure." She patted the chair next to her desk. "Sit right here. Just let me get these ragamuffins out to the playground and I'll be back in two shakes of a lamb's tail."

The rowdy boys flew out the door making annoying boy noises. Sunny knew they'd come in from recess all sweaty and smelling like dead fish. Bitty, her best friend gave her a worried look but followed the rest of their friends outside.

"Okay," Ms. Hamilton said as she pulled her desk chair close to Sunny and took her hand. "Tell me what's happening. Did you get up too late for your mom to fix your hair?

That's all it took for the tears to start, and once they did Sunny couldn't do anything to stop them. The next thing she knew she was in her teacher's lap.

"Now, now," Mrs. Hamilton said, rubbing small circles on Sunny's back. "Let it all out. Sometimes we just need a good cry." She grabbed a handful of tissues and handed them to Sunny. "I have a little girl with pretty blond curls like yours. She's in the third grade. Her name is Lolly."

"I know," Sunny said with a sniff. She'd cried so much her nose was running and the hiccups had started.

"Can you tell me what's happening?"

Sunny nodded and then it all spilled out. "My

mama didn't come home last night. And I think something's happened to Mrs. Burke, my babysitter. She didn't come over last night, and she wouldn't leave me alone. I'm really scared."

"You stayed by yourself all night?"

Sunny nodded, even though she was afraid she might be in trouble. Would the cops come and get her, too?

"Blow your nose." Ms. Hamilton looked sad. "I'm leaving for a second, but I'll be right back. Is that okay?"

"Yeah." Was it a mistake to tell her teacher? What was going to happen to her?

That question was answered when Mrs. Hamilton came back and took her to the principal's office. All kinds of people were scurrying around—there was even a policeman.

"Am I in trouble?" She was sitting in her teacher's lap.

"Absolutely not." Marci Hamilton smoothed Sunny's hair. "Talking to me was exactly the right thing to do. Mr. Bayliss, our principal, is a good man. He'll get this all sorted out."

Mr. Bayliss was huddled in the corner with some people who looked important. They were all wearing suits, except one woman who kept glancing at Sunny. She knew they were talking about her, but what were they saying and where was Mama?

It felt like she'd been in the principal's office for hours. But it probably wasn't as long as she thought because the bell for the end of school hadn't rung. And then the people in suits shook Mr. Bayliss's hand and left.

"I know things are confusing." He leaned over to wipe the tears running down Sunny's cheek. "We're going to take a little trip and then I'll explain everything. Mrs. Hamilton is going with us. Is that okay?"

Sunny nodded, not sure that she had a choice. And before she knew what was happening, Mr. Bayliss was holding her hand and they were standing on the porch of the prettiest house in town. When she and Mama walked to the grocery store they'd stop at the white picket fence and admire the yellow house with the green shutters. Then Mama would say, "One day honey, we'll live like that."

Sunny didn't quite believe her, but here she was standing on a front porch that was bigger than their whole trailer. Then it hit her like a ton of bricks. This was an orphanage! *No, No, No Way!* But where did little kids go when their parents went missing. Sunny had a death grip on her school bag. An orphanage didn't sound like her idea of a good time.

Don't, don't start bawling. Sunny was concentrating so hard she didn't quite get what Mr. Bayliss was saying. She did hear the door chime as it echoed through the house.

Sunny jumped backward when the door creaked open revealing a woman who was almost as round as she was tall. She had the prettiest smile on her chubby face.

"Lands sakes child, come in, come in. I'm Cora," she said as she called back over her shoulder. "Miss Anna Belle, Miss Eugenie our little guest is here."

"Mosey on back to the kitchen now, ya hear. I

have a fresh pot of coffee brewing and some chocolate chip cookies right out of the oven." She winked at Sunny. "I bet you like cookies, don't you?"

Sunny managed a nod. At this point even a small smile was impossible, so she was grateful the woman kept up the chatter. That way she didn't have to talk.

Cora led the way down the wide center hall to a kitchen at the back of the house. And what a kitchen! She'd seen a place like this in a magazine— gleaming copper pans were hanging over an island at least the size of Hawaii and the red brick floor was spotless.

"Sit down and I'll get those cookies. My, oh my, you're going to love my goodies." Cora toddled over to the stove and flipped the cookies from the baking sheet to a cooling rack. "Miss Anna Belle and Miss Eugenie will be down in a second. They've been fussin' over that room for hours."

Almost simultaneous to her proclamation, a wiggly mass of white fur with a black button nose jumped in Sunny's lap and bathed her face in puppy kisses. She couldn't help herself; a giggle bubbled up. No matter how bad things got, she couldn't resist a puppy.

"Looks like you've met Ruffles." Sunny recognized that slow southern drawl—it was Miss Carpenter, one of the fifth grade teachers. She was tiny and blond, like Mama, but older.

"I don't know if you remember me, I'm Anna Belle Carpenter," she said, squatting down to stroke Ruffles' fur. "My sister Eugenie will be here in a minute."

Miss Anna Belle hugged Mrs. Hamilton. "Marci

Ann DeFee

is my second cousin, or something. Anyway, she's family," she told Sunny and then shook Mr. Bayliss's hand. "It's been quite a day, hasn't it?"

He nodded. "That it has."

"Would you all like a glass of tea?"

"I'd love one. I'm parched." Mr. Bayliss said and Mrs. Marci nodded.

Miss Anna Belle scooted off and returned with a tray of drinks. She gently pushed a lock of hair off Sunny's face. "Cora takes good care of us. If you ever need anything, you can always ask her. And as you can tell, she makes a mean cookie."

What was the lady talking about? It was all so confusing! Sunny's trailer was clear across town, why would she make the trip to get a cookie?

"I can't stay. Mama will be worried when she gets home and I'm not there." Sunny could tell from the looks on the grown-ups faces that something bad was going on. "Really, I can walk home. You don't even have to drive me."

"Don't you worry, not one little bit. We'll tell your mama where you are." The voice belonged to a tall man with a kind smile and a huge gun planted on his hip. His companion was also tall, and she was one of the most beautiful creatures Sunny had ever seen.

The dark-haired woman leaned over to speak to Sunny. "You're going to stay with us for a while. I'm Miss Eugenie and this is Sheriff Madison. Would you like to sit in my lap while I tell you something?"

"No, ma'am. I'm just fine where I am." The news was going to be terrible. Sunny knew that as well as she knew her own name. Would it go away if she ignored it?

When Miss Eugenie and the sheriff gave each other another one of those grown-up looks, Sunny realized her life was about to change. More tears escaped and rolled down her cheeks.

"Sunny, sweetie," Miss Eugenie said taking her hand. "Your mother has been in an accident and she's in the hospital. And Mrs. Burke had a heart attack last night. She wasn't able to tell anyone about you so we didn't know you were home by yourself until this morning. Do you understand what I'm telling you?"

Sunny nodded. She really wished she could stop crying but she couldn't.

"You'll be staying with us. Would that be okay with you?"

All Sunny could manage was a nod. She really didn't want to spend the night at home alone. "Can I see her?" she couldn't help ending her question with a sniff.

"As soon as she feels better we'll take you to the hospital," the sheriff assured her. "But for now you'll be safe and cozy here with Miss Anna Belle and Miss Eugenie."

Although the words should have been comforting, the expression on his face was grim, but maybe that was how he always looked.

"Mama doesn't know these people. And she's always told me not to talk to strangers."

The Sheriff gave Mr. Bayliss another one of those looks.

"Sweetie." Uh-oh. A principal never called a kid "sweetie."

"Your mother knows and trusts me, and I

11

certainly wouldn't ask you to do something she wouldn't like. She knows Mrs. Hamilton, and Mrs. Hamilton is part of Miss Anna Belle and Eugenie's family."

"Okay, I guess," Sunny admitted reluctantly.

"Great, now that's settled."

Miss Eugenie smiled as she took Sunny's hand. "Why don't you bring Ruffles with you and we'll show you your room. If you'd like, Ruffles would be happy to sleep with you."

Miss Anna Belle and Miss Eugenie kept talking as they led the way upstairs to a bedroom so grand that Sunny was sure she'd stepped into a fairy tale. It was a little girl's dream come true with a four-poster bed, yellow flowered wallpaper and a sea of white eyelet.

Sunny was so confused. This room obviously belonged to a princess, and princesses didn't live in mobile home parks.

That was the beginning of the rest of Sunny McAllister's life. Several days later, the sheriff, Miss Eugenie and Miss Anna Belle took her to the hospital. Sunny stood in her mother's room watching the equipment beep and buzz. Her heart dropped to the tips of her toes. Mama wasn't coming home. She'd been hit by a car while she was running home after she'd heard that Mrs. Burke had had a heart attack.

"Mama's dying, isn't she?" Sunny had to ask the question even though she knew her heart would break when she heard the answer.

Miss Anna Belle made soothing little circles on her palm. "Yes, sweetheart, I'm afraid she is. But she knows we'll take good care of you. Remember how she said she loves you, and she wants you to live with us and have a happy life?"

"Yes," Sunny managed to answer through her tears.

"That's because she knows we'll do everything we can to make you happy. Right, sister?"

Miss Eugenie nodded and gave Sunny one of her slow, beautiful smiles.

"We'll never replace your mother, but we are so happy you'll be living with us," Miss Anna Belle said.

And with the innocence and wisdom of childhood, Sunny realized that everything would be all right. Much later she learned that Anna Belle and Eugenie's petition for guardianship had been expedited through the court system. Things like that happened in small towns, and it was especially fortunate that Anna Belle and Eugenie's cousin was the superior court judge.

After Eugenie married Sheriff Dave Madison and moved into the house next door, Anna Belle took over as Sunny's primary guardian. Later Anna Belle also married and the sisters decided it was time to make the adoption permanent. Since Anna Belle and her husband Joe Nunn were living in the Carpenter family home, they decided to become Sunny's official parents.

As much as Sunny loved and missed her mother, she experienced a wonderful childhood in the arms of her adoptive family. She had two beloved sets of parents, a family, friends and a wonderful new life.

But she'd love her mama forever and as big as the whole wide world.

Chapter 1

Sunny resisted the urge to beat her head on the three-way mirror. At five foot nothing and a hundred pounds soaking wet, everything she tried on made her look like she was playing dress-up. Fashion designers obviously didn't cater to folks who were built more like Peter Pan than Sofia Vergara.

Sunny glared at the pair of three-inch stilettos in the corner. Combine those instruments of torture with the pink sequined number that would be too long for Heidi Klum, and you could see where this was going. Shopping had to be one of the seven levels of hell, but giving up wasn't an option. Sunny had a wedding to attend; and by gosh, she planned to be a babe-a-licious if it killed her. However, if today was any indication, her demise might be slow and exceedingly painful.

Using the door as a shield, she peeked out to get her cousin's attention. "Liza, bring me something else. No more sequins, no more bare midriffs and no more ruffles. I need classy and short, very short."

A few seconds later the door popped open and Lily, cousin number two, flew in with another armload of gowns. Lily's fraternal twin, Liza, was right on her heels. Lily Walker and Liza Henderson were as physically dissimilar as the sun and the moon. Liza was petite with dark hair and big brown eyes. She was gorgeous in an exotic kind of way. Lily was tall, blond, voluptuous, and Marilyn Monroe beautiful. Their mom, Cecilia was Anna Belle and Eugenie's sister.

"Try these on. Swear to goodness, we've looked

at every size two in Houston." Lily waved a hand in the air as she plopped on the padded bench. "I think size two should be illegal, but that's neither here nor there." She tossed Sunny a small package.

"With that black lamé number you'll need these."

"What is this?" Sunny ripped open the wrapping and held up two flesh-colored half-mooned shaped bra cups—just the cups, nothing else.

"They're supposed to be adhesive," Liza offered. "If you hook them together, they give you cleavage."

Sunny responded with an unladylike snort. "Cleavage? Pulzee, a girl with A-minus bazooms does not now, nor will she ever, have cleavage."

"Shut up and put 'em on. This—" Liza held up the gown "—doesn't have a back."

Sunny sighed as she rubbed the bridge of her nose. "You guys are troupers." They'd accompanied her through every boutique and department store at the Galleria, Houston's glitziest shopping center. Plus, they'd endured a sea of sequins, silk, linen, tulle and something that suspiciously resembled colored cellophane. "No foolin', I appreciate you giving up a Saturday to do this."

"Are you kidding?" Lily gave Sunny a playful punch on the arm. "We have a vested interest in making sure the jerk's tongue hangs out when he gets a gander at you."

The jerk in question was Walter Harrington, Sunny's ex-husband. He was also the best-man for the upcoming festivities.

"I still have that hideous lavender bridesmaid

dress from your wedding," Liza tossed in that painful reminder.

Sunny didn't mention the fact her wedding dress resided in a trunk in the attic. Her family assumed that when she and Walter called it quits, she'd ditched everything associated with her ill-fated nuptials.

Wrong. Not that she still hankered for him. On the contrary—her favorite fantasy included a thousand fleas infesting his armpits. She'd kept the dress merely as a reminder to be very careful in the relationship game. But considering she hadn't had a date in a month of Sundays, her chances of getting involved in a male-female thingy were slim to none.

Talk about depressing.

But, back to the mission at hand—finding the perfect dress. The black-sequined number wasn't *even* in the ballpark. Not only was it backless, and virtually frontless, it was short enough to be a tennis skirt—minus the bloomers.

"Classy, I want classy with just a hint of sexy." Her proclamation drew dual eye-rolls from Lily and Liza.

Sunny couldn't blame them; she realized she was being difficult. This high-end boutique was not only well out of her price range, it was also her last resort. As the owner and operator of the Double Date Salon and Pet Grooming Spa in Port Serenity, Texas, she wasn't exactly rolling in money.

However, if she could find an outfit that would make Walter rue the day he'd dumped her, she'd be willing to strip down naked and whistle Dixie in the town square. Not that she thought she could make more than a buck fifty doing a striptease—heck, half the girls in the sixth grade had more curves than she did.

"Ladies, I found something in our new inventory." The sales clerk sounded almost as frenzied as Sunny felt.

Not expecting much, Sunny opened the door and encountered Nirvana in the form of pale pink silk suit—short, short skirt, camisole top and form-fitting jacket. The color was ideal for her platinum-blond hair and emerald-green eyes. It was love at first sight.

"Perfect."

Sunny didn't realize the dress was simply the starting point. She had to have shoes, a lacy push-up bra, the perfect earrings and a twenty-dollar pair of hosiery.

"I'd kill for a margarita." Liza uttered that sentiment as the three ladies left the boutique laden down with bags.

"Amen to that one. Dinner's on me and we're not going to a diner," Sunny said. "What do you guys think about the Prime Steakhouse?" It was expensive, but it was the least she could do for her two best friends.

"Whoo, hoo!" The twins expressed their approval in unison.

Sunny was debating between a strawberry daiquiri and a pina colada but finally decided to go for pink. "I want a little umbrella in it," she instructed the waiter.

He was cute, young and best of all, he had a sexy wink. "Sure, the drinks will be right up."

Sunny flopped back on the leather seat. She was exhausted, her feet hurt and her spiky hairdo had long since passed trendy and was rapidly heading toward dumpy. Not to mention she was working on a raging headache. Fortunately, or unfortunately, her cousins didn't look much better.

"I can't wait until Walter swallows his tongue. His newest squeeze is something of a woofer," Liza said, adding a laugh.

"Don't talk about my clients like that," Sunny said with a chuckle. "I can't believe how fast my business has grown since we added the grooming service. It's only been a little over two years and for the last couple of months we've been booked solid."

"I think your idea is incredibly clever," Liza said. "You can get a stylish make-over while your doggie best friend can enjoy the same kind of pampering at the grooming spa. Penny has to call for reinforcements every time I take Tulip in for her grooming."

"A Great Dane, no matter how cute, should not be named Tulip." Lily addressed her remark to her sister.

"And you think a teacup poodle with the moniker of Bubba is appropriate? I'm surprised you don't make him wear one of those collars with studs," Liza replied. This was an on-going conversation between the two sisters.

"You think Tulip hates a bath," Sunny said, cutting the discussion of dog names short. "You should see what happens when Police Chief Lolly Delacroix's dog Harvey shows up. That dog has enough hair for a grizzly bear. Everything in the grooming parlor is wet once Penny gets finished."

"And speaking of Lolly, that husband of hers is

one fine specimen." Lily did a mock wipe of her forehead."

Sunny nodded. "Too bad he's taken and his wife wears a gun."

"There is that," Liza said. "And Lily, you are married."

"Married, but not blind."

"Here are your drinks, ladies."

"Saved by the daiquiri with the umbrella," Liza said, eliciting laughs from her relatives.

Chapter 3

"Are you drowning your sorrows, or are you just really thirsty?" The speaker laughed as he slapped Landry Valliere IV on the back.

Landry glanced at the row of empty beer bottles. His law partner, Colby Wharton, was one of the biggest wiseacres in New Orleans, but this time he'd hit the nail on the head. Landry *had* been drowning his sorrows. It was a good thing his house was only a few blocks away; at least he could stumble home without being arrested.

"I don't consider it any of your business, but I was trying to formulate a plan for world peace," Landry proclaimed as he took another long swallow. His favorite bar, the Hair of the Hound, was the watering hole for a number of well-heeled citizens who called the upscale neighborhood of the Garden District home. The owner had transported an entire English pub lock, stock and tap from a village in the Cotswold's. It featured dark paneling, battle-scarred tables, the vague scent of wood smoke and eight hundred different brands of beer. Although Landry didn't intend to sample all eight hundred, he did plan to wade through quite a few of the brews.

"I'm getting a mixed message here." Colby waved his hand indicating the empty bottles. "You won the case this afternoon. However, from the looks of this mess you'd think you lost."

"I should have. The senator's punk kid was guilty as sin. When the jury announced the verdict, he

had the gall to giggle and wink at me. He winked at

me!"

"We're criminal defense attorneys. Sometimes we're responsible for getting guilty people off. It's the nature of the game. Don't you remember what they said in law school? Everyone has the right to a good defense.

Colby didn't bother to elaborate on the fact that Wharton and Valliere was the best and most expensive law firm in New Orleans, including the surrounding areas of Louisiana and Mississippi.

Landry absently arranged the empty bottles by height. "Did you know the man he ran into had a house full of kids?"

The teenager had admitted he'd been drinking and speeding when he T-boned a cab, killing the driver. Although Landry got the boy off on a technicality, he'd bet his Porsche that within a week the spoiled brat would be sloshed and behind the wheel again. And why not? If the kid got into trouble, Daddy would get him off, just like he'd done this time.

"I hated the case." Landry proclaimed, as he grabbed a handful of peanuts. He had to get something in his stomach besides alcohol, or he'd regret it in the morning.

Colby put his chin on his fist and stared at his business partner. "You know what your problem is?"

"Nope, but I'm sure you're about to tell me." Landry's snide comment was lost on his friend.

"Bet your sweet butt, I am. You're suffering from burnout. Up to now you've had it too easy. You went to the best schools in the country and you have a trust fund that equals the GNP of several third-world nations. You have good looks, brains and a bloodline that dates back to the War of 1812. You have it made, but you feel there's something missing. Something you need to experience."

"Your point being?"

Colby gave him the stare that had always been a prelude to trouble. "My point is that you need to get in touch with your inner 'Joe Six-Pack'."

"Like your family's poor," Landry said with a snort.

"You're right. But I grew up in a small town so I knew people from a variety of backgrounds. My best friend's old man was in jail for armed robbery and his mother worked in a convenience store. For them, keeping the electricity on was a challenge."

Colby paused as if pondering the situation. "In fact, watching them scrimp and save to pay an attorney was one of the reasons I was so adamant about establishing our pro bono program. And with that in mind, I have a bet," he said with a mischievous grin.

Uh oh! They'd started making wagers when they were roommates in law school and invariably Landry ended up on the losing side.

"What?" Even giving voice to the question was dangerous.

"You remember all those stories I told you about Port Serenity."

How could Landry forget? Every time Colby had more than a couple of beers in his belly he prattled on about his hometown, Port Serenity, Texas. It was the last place on the planet Landry wanted to visit.

"Yeah?" he answered.

Colby leaned back, a smirk dancing across his

face.

A smirk! This had all the earmarks of something seriously bad.

"Here are the stakes. If I win, you coerce some our bar association colleagues to do more pro bono work, *and* you fix me up with your sister. Every time I ask her out, she comes up with a lame excuse. How many times can a woman paint her nails?

It was Landry's turn to smirk. "Wonder what Kristen's thinking? Could it be that she remembers the one and only date you guys had? The time you tied one on and ended up puking on the sidewalk...? Hmm. Do you suppose that turned her off?"

"I was nervous. Use your charm to convince her I'm a reformed man. You can do it."

"I don't know." Landry shook his head, simply to tease his friend. Colby was one of the nicest guys in town.

"If you win, we'll change the name of the firm to Valliere and Wharton. We'll do the letterhead, the business cards, the whole deal."

Convincing their colleagues to do anything that would impact their bottom line would be challenging, and Kristen would rather date Godzilla than go out with Colby, but the idea of changing the name of the firm *was* appealing. The only reason it was currently named Wharton and Valliere was the result of a bad coin toss, so a bet was sort of karmic.

"Okay, what are you proposing?"

"I want you to start over, at least for a little while. See if you can make it without anything but a few bucks in your pocket. That way you can experience how some of our more unfortunate clients live." The more he talked, the more Colby got into the spirit of the game.

"Here's the deal. You show up in Port Serenity with only two-hundred-dollars to your name. It has to last you a full month or until you get a job. No credit cards, no car, and no fair using your education or connections. There'll be just two hundred dollars standing between you and starvation."

Of all the wacky ideas Colby had ever come up with—and they were legion—this was the topper, but Landry decided to play along.

"Okay, I have a couple of questions. First, what about your parents? What are they going to think if they see me walking the streets of Port Serenity?"

"No problem. They're on an around-the-world cruise. They won't be back for a couple of months."

One excuse down—one to go. "What about our workload? Can you guys handle everything without me?"

Colby gave him one of those "are you kidding" looks. "We've tied up most of our big cases, and besides that, you haven't had a vacation in years," he said. "I think it's more important for you to regain some enthusiasm for our profession than for us to take on a new case. So yes, we'll do fine without you for a month or so."

There was something to be said for renewing his professional passion. "Does that hometown of yours have a McDonalds?" If all else failed, surely he could get a job at Mickey D's.

"Nope," Colby said, grinning ear to ear. "And here's the rest of the deal. At the end of June there's a big party put on by the Historical Society. If you can get invited to that—and going as a waiter doesn't count—you win. If you don't, I'm the victor."

How hard could it be to get invited to a party? Landry was on the New Orleans' society A-list. But they were discussing *Port Serenity, Texas,* and he had a suspicion he had just signed on to the biggest sucker bet of all time. Colby had had the hots for Kristen a very long time.

"I'll give you fair warning, a historical society party invitation is something folks work years to get. They don't invite just *anyone.* Even as handsome as you are, you'll have a hard time cracking that nut."

Damn him! Colby knew there wasn't anything like a dare to get Landry's juices flowing.

He tipped his bottle in a salute to friendship and a good bet. "You're on, buddy. Here's to the big party."

Chapter 4

Yep, Landry had been snookered. What in hell had he been thinking? He had a law practice, a home and a life. So what was he doing on a Greyhound bus sharing a seat with a guy who had only a marginal acquaintance with personal hygiene?

The whole thing had been pretty much of a lark until he landed in Houston—that was when he'd put two and two together and got a whoppin' big six. The inventory of his personal possessions included a driver's license (no way could he buy a car—shoot, he couldn't afford a spark plug), the aforementioned two hundred dollars (and forty-seven cents), and a duffle bag containing a couple of pairs of well-worn jeans and some old T-shirts (thanks to Colby's packing skills). With that wardrobe, he'd be lucky to get a job washing dishes.

"This is it," his seat companion said. The man had come out of his stupor and was pointing at something out the window.

"What?" Landry asked.

"That's Port Serenity, the place you said you were going."

"Oh, yeah, thanks." Landry picked up his bag as the bus belched to a stop in front of a run-down hotel. The peeling paint and listing veranda notwithstanding, Landry could see that at one time, the Palm Inn had been a bastion of gentility and big-hat tea parties. It must have fallen on hard times because now it doubled as the bus

station, a Western Union office and a coffee shop.

He grimaced as he stepped off the vehicle into a wall of heat, humidity and wind. Landry wiped the sweat off his forehead.

Gut up, you can do this. And that quickly became his mantra.

The inside of the terminal was only slightly better than the outside. The ancient air conditioner wasn't keeping up with the heat. Landry strolled to the coffee shop and sat down on one of the cracked vinyl seats at the counter.

"What can I do for ya?" The waitress was friendly, but definitely had that "rode hard and put away wet" look.

"A big iced tea, please."

"Sure enuf, hon." She was back in a few moments with a glass that contained at least a gallon of amber liquid.

"Anything to eat?" she asked.

Actually, he'd love a cheeseburger, but his priorities were a job first and superfluous things like food second.

"Nope. Not right now. Thank you."

"Sure, hon. I can't blame you." The waitress hitched a hip up and leaned against the counter. "Lord in heaven, it's too hot to eat. We don't normally sweat like this until August."

"Really?"

"You ain't from around here, are you, sugar?"

"Nope. New Orleans."

"Always wanted to go there, but I've never been out of Texas. I went to Houston with my first husband." She tapped her front tooth. "Or was that my second?"

27

Did she really expect an answer?

"Oh, well, never mind. Let me know if you need anythin' else, ya hear?" She started to wipe the counter.

"Well, Mabel, there is one thing." Landry had noticed the nametag pinned to the front of her pink uniform. "Do you know anyone who needs an employee?"

"Depends. What do you know how to do?"

That was a good question. While Landry was intimately familiar with writs of habeas corpus, restraining orders and arraignment procedures, he couldn't list many practical skills.

"I don't know."

It obviously wasn't the answer Mabel was expecting. She scratched her head before speaking. "Seems like I heard that Danny down at the service station is looking for someone to change oil. Any guy worth his salt can do that."

Talk about a good way to impugn his manhood. He normally took his Porsche to the dealer for routine maintenance, so obviously auto mechanics wasn't one of his long suits. But how hard could it be?

"Where can I find Danny?"

Mabel pointed out the front door. "Take a right and go up past the courthouse, then turn left at statue of the crab. That's Main Street. Danny's place is two blocks up on the right. You can't miss it. It's the Valero station."

He probably could—miss it, that is, especially since he'd die of heat prostration before he got there.

"Thanks." Landry finished the tea and left a hefty tip. That habit would have to come to a screeching halt. "I'll tell him Mabel sent me."

"Sure enuf, hon, you do that."

No wonder people in this part of the world ambled; he'd only walked half a block, yet he felt like he'd been wrapped in Saran Wrap and put in a slow-bake oven. He was tempted to stick himself with a fork to see if he was done.

But when in Rome, etc., so he strolled down the tree-lined street appreciating the quaintness of his home for the next month. That is if he could find someplace to stay, a way to earn money and get something decent to eat.

That proved to be easier said than done.

The stitched name on the shirt said Danny. The owner of the garment was beefy, bald and short-tempered. "If you don't know how to change oil, I can't use you." He made that statement right before he rolled back under a Chevy Impala that had seen better days.

Scratch that one. Three hours, Landry had also been turned down for a job at the Temptee Freeze (their work force was limited to young, nubile blonds), Dale's Supermarket (Ed's cousin had been hired to do the stocking), and as a dishwasher at the Urban Diner. That one really frosted him. First of all, there was nothing even remotely urban about the place; and second, the middle-aged female owner made some crude remark about his rear end and then said that he was too "purty." Claimed he'd be a distraction to the waitresses.

The folks in Port Serenity were obviously *not* familiar with sexual discrimination laws.

It was almost five o'clock, and things were

looking grim. No job, no lodging, and very little money—crap! The only bright spot in his day was that he was about to solve his hunger problem with a bag of day-old fried chicken and a thirty-two ounce Big Gulp. He hoped to God it didn't kill him. The good news was that the entire meal had only set him back only a dollar seventy-five.

Landry had noticed a gazebo in the park next to the beach. There were benches, it was private and it seemed perfect for an impromptu picnic. And if he was really lucky, the cops wouldn't bust him for loitering. At least if he went to jail he'd get three hots and a cot—and wasn't that a pitiful thought.

Even though the chicken was greasy and cold, he cleaned the bones like a buzzard dining on roadkill. When dusk brought a welcome breath of cool breeze, Landry kicked back and savored the sweet smell of newly cut grass and the sound of kids playing on the beach. It had been a long time since he'd felt so relaxed.

Perchance there was something to be said for the slow and easy rhythm of beach living...

Who did he think he was kidding? He was a city boy, through and through.

Landry briefly considered calling off the bet. Nope, he wasn't a quitter. And he'd rather face a nest of pit vipers than arrange a date between Kristen and Colby. Those two idiots were like oil and water.

So discounting the idea of losing the wager, Landry checked his limited assets. The meager number of bills in his hand-tooled Italian wallet was enough to make a grown man cry. Simply put—he needed a game plan ASAP, and the first item on that list was a flea-bag hotel, preferably minus the bed bugs. He tossed the empty bag into the garbage and went in search of a cheap motel.

Morning found him back at his favorite park bench munching on a half-dead banana and slugging back a quart of milk. He felt horrible. No wonder—he hadn't had *any* sleep. The mattress was as hard as a Mayan sacrificial altar, and the constant rhythmic banging on the wall next to his headboard was enough to induce permanent insomnia.

Landry was trying to figure out his options when he spied potential salvation. The hand lettered sign, "Shampoo Girl Wanted, Apply Within," was in the window of an establishment that screamed girly-girl. Everything from the pink-and-white striped awning, to the flowerboxes with trailing coral geraniums, to the Double Date written in gold script was frilly to the max.

Shampooing a bunch of strangers sounded about as appealing as cleaning portable loos, but Landry was desperate. He washed his own hair every morning. How hard could the job be?

Landry chugged the rest of the milk and marched across the street. In a thousand years of bad fantasies he'd never considered stooping to anything this ignominious; but hey, it was better than slopping hogs. Wearing his best courtroom smile, Landry strolled into Double Date. He'd charmed hundreds of jurors, so how difficult could it be to convince the owner of a salon in Podunk, Texas, to hire him.

Regrettably, the answer to that question, ladies and gentlemen of the jury, would probably be—pretty damned hard.

Chapter 5

"Okay ladies, we have a busy day and we're still short-handed, so—" Sunny paused "—if you'll just hang in with me I promise we'll get some help soon." Their daily staff meeting usually degenerated into a gossip fest. What did she expect when the "staff" consisted of her three wackiest friends?

Raylene Yarborough was the darling of the blue-haired set—that girl could process the tightest perm in Texas. And then there was Tallulah Tucker—just call her Toolie—an expatriate from a posh Houston salon and a favorite of the trendy gals. Not to mention Penny Warnicke, her groomer. She'd been a rodeo barrel racer in a previous life and could pick up a steer if necessary.

"Hon," Raylene said, popping her gum in rhythm to a Taylor Swift tune, "have you managed to round up a date for the wedding?"

Sunny sighed. Business always played second fiddle to chitchat and today wasn't any different.

"No, and how much shampoo do I need to order?"

"Really? Time's a wastin'." Raylene fluffed her already big hair. "Toolie, hon, do you know any eligible men?"

"How about conditioner?" Sunny asked, even though she knew that trying to change the subject would be like turning back the tide.

"Seriously? All the guys of my acquaintance, sort of, you know, like bat for the other team." Toolie raised her eyebrows for emphasis.

"All the guys I pal around with drive a six-pack

pickup and hanker for a chaw every now and then." That tidbit came from Penny.

"And everyone I know is or married or divorced a couple of times. I don't know which is worse," Raylene said.

"That's it! Read my lips. I *do not* need a date for the wedding. I don't mind going by myself."

Raylene, Toolie and Penny stared, astounded at their boss's audacious declaration.

"And don't look at me like that!" Aargh! The trio meant well, but when they started meddling they made her crazy.

"Holy cow, would you take a gander at that." Raylene had wandered over to the front window and was watching something, or someone, in the park across the street.

Toolie and Penny joined their friend. "Now that's what I call eye-candy," Toolie said.

"Sunny, come here, girl. You've got to see this." When Raylene put her mind to something she was like a pit bull gnawing on a bone.

"No! We have business to discuss."

Her employees were practically plastered to the window. "Well lookie, lookie. Oh, my goodness, I'm about to swoon." When Raylene fanned her face, Sunny realized she was fighting a losing battle.

"Are you sure you don't want a lookie-loo," Toolie taunted. "Great black hair and that bad-boy look you dig—T-shirt, tight jeans and scuffed boots. Yummy, yummy." She emphasized the point by licking her lips.

"Hush up. You two sound like you're in middle school."

"Ooh, dude. He just stood up and is he ever built," Toolie continued her running commentary.

Penny tossed in her two-cents. "I'd dump Coolie if I thought I had a fighting chance with that hunk."

"I'm havin' a flash of light." Raylene tapped a crimson nail on her forehead.

"What you're havin' is a stroke. Now, all of you get over here so we can finish our business. We have to get this shop open."

"I'm gonna run over and see if we can hire him to take you to the wedding."

"Over my dead body!" Sunny was about panic. They really were capable of pulling that kind of harebrained stunt.

"Great idea," Toolie agreed. "Make sure he has all his teeth. We can find him something to wear and make him presentable. With that bone structure and the right clothes, he'll look like a million bucks."

"No!" Sunny screeched. "I don't need a date, and if I did. . ." Her rant was interrupted in mid-stream by Raylene's next comment.

"Well, ladies, it looks like we're about to see him up close and personal. He's headin' this way."

"Good grief!" Sunny watched in fascination. It felt like everything was moving in slow motion.

The bell above the door tinkled its happy little greeting. Funny, Sunny thought, that used to seem cheerful, but now it sounded more like a psychotic elf banging on a tin can.

"Ladies," he said, with the slightest hint of a Southern accent. She got the impression that if he'd been wearing a cap, he would have tipped it.

"I think you might have a job for me."

Oh, boy. If he could bottle that grin he'd make a fortune. Then his comment hit Sunny. And if Raylene's bugged-out eyes were any indication, she'd received the same message. Toolie and Penny merely giggled.

"Uh, well, um, it's like this." Sunny had no clue what it was like. Although she'd graduated cum laude with a degree in English, she was being amazingly monosyllabic.

"Well, sugar, I don't think. . ."

The tall, dark and devastatingly handsome stranger interrupted Raylene. "I know I can do the job." He winked. "It can't be that hard, and I'm sure the ladies will love me."

On that note, Sunny almost swallowed her tongue. No way would she hop off to the wedding with a hired date—no matter how good looking. "I'm sorry I don't think so."

The man looked genuinely puzzled. "Is it because I'm a guy?"

"Huh?"

"Well, I mean, how hard can it be to give someone a shampoo? I'm a hard worker and I don't have many vices. How about this? I work free for a couple of days. That way you can try me out without it costing you a cent."

Glory Be! The guy was applying for the shampoo girl job. Talk about feeling like an idiot. Even more disturbing was the fact that Sunny found herself agreeing to his plan.

"You're on. Work today for free and then we can talk." Where had that come from? "Raylene, why don't you get all his particulars like name, address, social security number, etc?"

"Thanks, that's great," the man said with the now-familiar grin.

Sunny hesitated before she took the hand he offered. Her stomach did a backflip when she touched him. Somehow, some way, this decision was going to change her life.

She hoped to goodness it wouldn't be a huge mistake.

Chapter 6

Even though the day had started out on a sucky note—her alarm didn't go off, the garbage disposal backed up, and her cat left a dead mouse on back porch—and despite the fact that every woman who walked in the salon was drooling over the new employee, Sunny was determined to maintain her dignity and decorum. That is until Raylene dropped the bomb—their shampoo guy was homeless. What next, an infestation of cicadas?

"Homeless? What makes you think that?"

"How about the fact he's using the Palm Inn as an address?"

"Oh, my word!" Sunny exclaimed. "What if he's wanted by the law? We could be arrested as accomplices, or accessories after the fact, or whatever."

"You're a weird woman," Raylene informed her. "There's nothing wrong with that man except he's down on his luck. My intuition tells me he's perfectly fine, and as you know," she preened, "my female antenna is never wrong."

"That's why you've been married three times?"

Raylene stuck out her tongue. "Don't get smart with me, girl. Just look at that." She was referring to the gorgeous man who was chatting up Viola Horatio while he washed her shoe-polish black hair.

"Merciful heavens, how much shampoo is he using? Look at all those bubbles!" Sunny exclaimed.

"Not to worry. If he makes Morticia happy that makes me downright giddy. She's actually smiling and that old bat hasn't cracked a grin in the last decade."

Sunny suppressed a giggle. When Raylene was right, she was right. Viola Horatio had the tightest "cheeks" in all of Texas.

For years they'd been trying to convince her to go for a color that was a bit closer to nature—but so far, no luck. She liked her Morticia look, complete with a streak of snow-white hair.

Viola and her husband Percy were the Mutt and Jeff of Port Serenity, and they were frequently the hottest topic of gossip. Their latest escapade involved her chasing him around the city park with a skillet. Rumor had it she'd found him kissing the choir director in the basement of the Methodist church. That was when she decided to play some "Amazing Grace" on his noggin.

Poor Mr. Horatio.

"How are you doing, Miz Thornton?" Sunny asked, greeting her next client. She was about to snap the black plastic cape around the woman's wrinkled neck, but stopped when she heard a noise up front.

"I'll be right back," she said, patting Mrs. Thornton's thin shoulder. Some of the seniors tended to get upset when anything deviated from the norm, and whatever was happening in the reception area sounded like it was way outside the ordinary.

"Hey, yo, open that cash drawer!" The man's slurred demand was almost obliterated by the sound of Toolie squealing.

Damn, that girl was loud!

Landry was trying to decipher the difference between a lanolin hair mask and a deep conditioner when he heard a scream. Mrs. Horatio jumped straight out of the chair.

Something bad was going down. If this had been New Orleans, he would have automatically assumed it was a drive-by shooting.

"Stay where you are," Landry instructed, sprinting toward the front of the salon. What he saw when he rounded the corner was not good, not good at all. This was Mayberry, USA; so what was a dude doing with a tea towel over his face and waving a gun?

Robbing the joint, that's what. Crap!

When Toolie screamed, Landry slid to an immediate halt. He couldn't go unprepared into the middle of a potential bloodbath. He had to have a plan.

Think. Think. Think.

Weapons? Nope. The most lethal thing he had in his arsenal was a can of hairspray.

Brains? Yep. He had plenty, and considering the situation, he needed every particle of gray matter he could muster.

"Here, here take it all." The voice belonged to his cute little blond boss. How had she made it to the front so fast?

Toolie finally stopped screeching. Thank you God!

Landry took another peek and noticed that even though Sunny was shoving a handful of bills at the robber, he was still screaming obscenities. The guy was a meth head, no doubt about it. At best, they could be treacherously erratic; at their worst, they were homicidal. It all added up to a dangerous situation.

"Um, what are we going to do?" Raylene

whispered.

Landry had been so focused on the crime that he almost jumped out of his skin when she tapped him on the shoulder. It took a few seconds for his heart to resume its normal cadence. A wise man one said that necessity was the mother of invention, and this situation fell into the category of a "mother."

Landry put a finger to his lips in the universal sign for silence and waved the ladies, who were creeping forward, back to the rear of the salon.

"Call 911," he whispered to a woman who had enough foil in her hair to pick up radio waves. She nodded and scooted toward Sunny's office.

Landry grabbed the fire extinguisher and was heading toward the front of the shop when he realized he wasn't alone. He glanced over his shoulder and found Raylene right behind him.

"I'm going with you," she mouthed.

"No," he mouthed back.

"Think again, buster."

And that's how Landry ended up with a sidekick who looked more like Dolly Parton than Barney Fife.

Damn—at least Barney had *one* bullet.

"You make a commotion to get his attention while I crawl behind the counter. Then I'll spray him with this." He indicated the extinguisher. "You okay with that?"

Raylene nodded.

The situation was rapidly escalating out of control. No matter what Sunny said or did, the man became more agitated. Please God, he wouldn't start shooting. Waiting for the cops was no longer an option.

Raylene tapped Landry and whispered, "Now?"

"Now," he replied as he got down on his hands and knees to make the crawl across the floor. It was no more than ten feet, but it looked as broad as the Sahara.

Although Landry didn't regularly darken the doors of his neighborhood church; this situation called for some praying. Heavenly intervention was a good thing—especially when he was dealing with a potential hostage situation, and that's exactly what was going to happen if a deputy dog stumbled in the door.

Landry gave his accomplice the high sign and readied himself.

Sunny was attempting to calm things when chaos broke out. At least that's what it sounded like. Actually, it was Raylene beating on something and screaming like a banshee. What *did* she think she was doing? Agitating this guy was not going to help, not when he was waving a gun.

Then Sunny spied her newest employee crawling toward a glass counter containing hair products. Okay, she got it—frontal distraction, rear attack.

"What the hell, man?" the meth head muttered as he redirected his gun toward the back of the shop.

It was now or never, Sunny thought as she grabbed the pepper spray from under the counter. Toolie had a deer-in-the-headlights look as she watched Sunny shake the can.

"Hey, stupid, this way," Sunny yelled. When the bad guy spun around, she let him have it right in the face. He let out a horrendous scream, prompting Landry to jump from behind the counter and finish him off with a dousing of chemical foam.

It was teamwork at its finest. The icing on the cake was when Raylene and Penny decided to give the old boy a big-time whoopin'.

"I got the gun," Landry said, holding up the weapon. "I think he messed with the wrong folks."

"No kiddin'," Raylene agreed, as she plopped her ample rear on the intruder's body and then bounced a couple of times for good measure. "We've got woman power." She polished her nails on her chest and grinned.

"Ever thang okay in here?" Patrolman Booty Carter asked as he strolled in the front door. In a previous life Booty had been one of the best tackles in Port Serenity High football history. In this incarnation, his girth leaned more toward paunch than punch.

"We're okay. He's not doing as well," Sunny said, indicating the man on the floor.

"Hey, Miss Raylene. Whatcha got down there?"

The perp groaned when she bounced again. "This guy tried to rob us, rob us! I want you to throw the book at him, ya hear me."

"Yes, ma'am, we'll see what we can do." Booty replied, snapping the cuffs on the perp.

"Take me in. Now, man." The whiny request came from Raylene's captive.

Booty was wearing a great big grin until Landry spoke.

"Officer, I have the gun." He held the firearm out with two fingers.

Police procedure in Port Serenity was as different from New Orleans as night and day. Back home if the cops encountered a guy with a gun he would have been spread eagle on the ground before he could blink. In the Port Serenity scenario, the policeman simply took the weapon.

As nice as the good-old-boy network might seem, police work here was a bit too casual for Landry's taste. That type of negligence got people killed.

Chapter 7

"Oh. My. Gawd," Toolie squealed. "That was so... that was so." She couldn't seem to finish her thought before falling into the nearest chair.

"Is it okay for us to come out now?" The disembodied voice belonged to Joynelle Tucker, the high-school principal's wife. The woman with the small sheets of tinfoil plastered all over her head looked timidly around the corner. "We called 911 but we never heard a siren." She was soon joined by a group of females in various stages of the hair dressing process.

"What happened?" one of the ladies asked.

"Lord have mercy," Raylene said, putting a motherly arm around Joynelle's shoulders. "Honey, we've got to get that stuff out of your hair. It's gonna burn right up." She led Joynelle off to wash out the highlighting bleach. "Mr. Landry and Miss Sunny took him right down. I swear, girl, I've never seen anything quite like it." She emphasized her point with a giggle. "After they got him down, I sat on him until Booty Carter got around to getting his fat butt over here."

Her comment sent the ladies into a spate of giggles. And why not? Successful termination of the fight-or-flight response generally created a euphoric effect.

"You did great," Toolie said, folding Sunny in a hug. "And you handsome dog, I'd select you for my team any day of the week and twice on Sunday." She gave Landry a wink.

"I second that," Mrs. Horatio declared, leading the rest of the ladies in a round of applause that was accompanied by catcalls, whistles and leers.

Landry was used to receiving appreciative looks from ladies; however, this felt like a whole new ball game. He was afraid he had acquired a rabid fan club. Although if it got him invited to the historical society party, that might not be such a bad thing.

"Do you know who that was?" The question came from Mrs. Laverne Hightower, an octogenarian and archivist of most of the town's secrets.

Landry had a premonition her explanation would bowl him over. But he had to ask. "Who was it?"

Although Mrs. Hightower wasn't an inch over four foot ten she somehow managed to command the attention of a room full of overexcited women.

"He was that old fart Crumpy Hardaway's grandson." She emphasized her identification by slamming her hands on her skinny hips.

Landry looked to Sunny; however, it was obvious from the look on her face that she was clueless.

"Who are you talking about?" Leave it to Raylene to get to the point.

Mrs. Hightower snorted. "Crumpy is the head of that clan of rednecks that lives out in the swamp. They've had their knickers in a twist about Miss Sunny's family for years. My great-granny said they got to squabbling over the deed to some land. Crumpy's kin thought they got the short end of the stick, and the families have been enemies ever since. Wouldn't surprise me none if those boys weren't trying to start somethin' again. They're pure white trash and they don't have the good sense God gave a cockroach."

"I've never heard anything about a Hatfield and

McCoy feud involving my family," Sunny said and then decided to get control of the situation. "Okay, the excitement's over, so let's see if we can get this place back to normal."

"I have a great idea," Toolie said after she stopped shaking.

Sunny's friend was not at her best during a crisis. And this was by far worse than the time she over processed the preacher's wife's hair and it fell out in clumps. Remembering that event, and the stylist's somewhat unorthodox approach to the predicament, Sunny mentally did a big uh-oh. Toolie's ideas tended to be way, way, way out in left field.

"I think you should let Landry use the apartment upstairs," she said.

Oh, boy—Toolie wanted to give a homeless guy unlimited access to the building?

"Uh, well, uh…"

"I think it's a great idea," Raylene said. Darn, she'd always been a sucker for the bad- boy, hero type, and unfortunately, Landry fit that description to a T.

"Yes, that would be lovely." Leave it to Mrs. Horatio to express an opinion.

"Oh, yeah," Joynelle agreed.

Sunny didn't concur with either sentiment, but she was delighted to notice that Joynelle's hair hadn't been burned to a bloody crisp.

"I don't think…" She started to say "that's a good idea," but before she could complete the thought she was interrupted by a chorus of support for her newest employee.

"All right, all right. But—" she turned to Mr.

47

Gorgeous, who looked amazingly sheepish, "—this is temporary. One month only. And, if I don't like you as a tenant, you're out of there. Are we in agreement?"

"Yes, ma'am."

Chapter 8

Landry couldn't believe his luck. Adios and good riddance to the Palm Inn. He had a place to live—goodbye cockroaches, hello clean bathroom. And best of all, no more audible trysts in the next room.

His new digs were definitely on the Spartan side. The bed looked lumpy, but it was private and it was his, at least for a while. And a while was all he needed because the minute he won the bet, he was history. New Orleans never looked more alluring.

Landry unloaded his two sacks of newly purchased groceries. He was astonished at how tough it was to shop when you didn't have wheels. Oh, well, he was now the proud owner of most of the basics—toilet paper, bread, fruit, coffee, peanut butter and beer. It was also amazing how expensive everything seemed when one suddenly morphed into a penny-pincher who would make Scrooge look generous. God, what he wouldn't give for just one of his credit cards.

It's only a month; it's only a month—and with that in mind, Landry popped the top on one of his prize beers and leaned back to survey his kingdom. The Goodwill reject couch was scary and the toilet was cranky, but it was a port in a storm and all that nonsense.

Chaos reigned when Landry reported to work the next day. The phone was ringing off the wall, women were demanding entrance, and the salon wasn't even open.

"What's happening," he asked his new boss. Boy, was she cute, even considering the scowl.

"This...this is happening." She made an all-encompassing motion with her arms and then shot him a look that could curdle milk.

It took a few moments for Landry to process what she was talking about, and when he did he was astonished. The counters were loaded with baked goods—several plates of chocolate chip cookies, at least two pound cakes, pastries of every description, a big banana pudding-type thing, and even what looked like a pineapple upside-down cake.

"Did someone die?"

"No! Not unless you decide to kick the bucket," Sunny exclaimed before she stormed toward her office.

"What did I do?"

Raylene patted his hand. "Sugar, you didn't do a thing. Not a single thing. You're just the most handsome man to hit Port Serenity in a very long time."

"What?"

"This—" Raylene indicated the plethora of baked goods "—is a Texas girl's way of catching the eye of an eligible bachelor. And a few of these goodies came from overzealous mama's who want grandkids real bad."

"You have *got* to be kidding," Landry exclaimed, barely able to keep his mouth from dropping open.

"Nope, I'm as serious as a speeding ticket. Right, Toolie?"

Toolie held a chocolate chip cookie in one hand and a peanut butter morsel in her other fist. "Damned straight. And may I say, keep up the good work."

The phone rang again and Landry discovered that as of yesterday afternoon, appointments at Double

Date were at a premium. It seemed that single women all over town were clamoring for a cut, curl or color, and most of them wanted to bring in their pets for a make-over.

Landry was assessing the bake-off when Penny tapped him on the shoulder.

"I'm gonna need your help, big boy."

"Okay. You name it and I'm ready."

Penny giggled before getting down to business." "Police Chief Lolly and her daughter Amanda are coming in for a haircut and they're bringing Harvey."

"And Harvey is?"

Penny rolled her eyes. "He's a Newfoundland the size of a Shetland pony and to put it mildly, he's a terror when it comes to a bath."

"Is he mean?" Landry was a huge dog fan, but getting taken down by a behemoth would not be his preference.

"Naw, he's a sweetie, but plan to get really wet."

"That I can handle." Piece of cake, Landry thought.

First, good ole Harv refused to get in the tub, requiring some manhandling—or that would be dog-handling—a hundred and fifty pound pooch who planted his paws and refused to move. Weren't Newfie's supposed to be water dogs? Unfortunately no bothered to clue in Harvey—when he shook the entire room, including the human occupants, took a drenching.

"Holy cow!" Landry exclaimed. "Does this happen often?"

Penny laughed and shook her head. "I like to do the poodles."

Sunny knew exactly what had happened when she spied Landry heading for the apartment stairs. She really had to hire Penny some help.

Not only was the man eye candy—and wow, did he ever look good in a wet T-shirt—he could charm the birds out of the trees. Animal magnetism aside, Sunny's female intuition was jumping up and down waving red flags. Sure he was alluring, and sexy, and too yummy for words, but there was also something fishy about him. He wasn't your run-of-the-mill underachiever; so why *was* he working in her salon?

And what *exactly* was he doing in Port Serenity? The first thing that came to mind was he was running from the law. But he didn't seem the least bit intimidated by Booty so he probably wasn't a fleeing felon. That left—what? Getting the heck away from a vindictive wife. Trying to find his inner child? Get real!

The whole thing was giving her a headache. And the dingbats who worked for her didn't help matters. Every time Landry showed up they turned into giggling loons.

Not that Sunny could blame them. Just the sight of Landry Valliere was enough to make a normal girl drool. And she was she a one-hundred-percent normal American girl. At times of weakness he almost made her reassess her self-imposed celibacy.

Yikes! What *was* she thinking?

Chapter 9

Quit ogling the hired help, it's not professional, Sunny thought as she checked out his fine butt one last time. Women of all sizes and shapes were streaming into the salon demanding her staff's attention. Dogs of every size, shape and breed were wandering around butt-sniffing their friends. It was a three-ring circus—and as much as she hated to do it—it was time for her to head into the fray.

The day went by in a whirl of cuts and color. Sunny couldn't remember being quite that busy. Landry Valliere was drawing in women like bees to honey. One client had given him a suggestive up-and-down and slipped him her phone number before she'd sashayed out the door. Jeeze Louise!

Sunny plopped in her chair and waited for the last customer to leave. She was exhausted and she knew her employees were equally as tired.

"I have to have some help!" Penny declared as she dropped into the nearest chair.

Raylene fell into onto the adjacent stool. "My puppies are woofin'," she announced, taking off her shoe and rubbing her foot. "I think we could use a bit of libation. How about it?"

Toolie had finally finished a complicated series of cornrows and joined them. "Lord, that makes my hands hurt," she proclaimed, shaking her fingers in an attempt to restore circulation. "And definitely, I want a libation, if that's anything like an alcoholic drink."

Fortunately or unfortunately, as the case may be,

Raylene kept a pitcher of margarita mix in the refrigerator. She said it was for emergencies, and they all agreed this qualified.

"Where's Mr. Sexy?" Raylene asked as she handed out plastic glasses of lime-green liquid.

"I think he went to his apartment," Sunny said. "I wouldn't bet the farm on it, but I suspect he's not used to being around quite *that* many women or dogs."

"Can you blame him?" Toolie ended her question with a hoot of laughter. "They about drove me nuts, and I'm around them all the time."

"Let's get back to the important business." Raylene took a big swig of margarita. "The wedding is coming up on Saturday, and you, missy—" she pointed at Sunny "—are dateless."

"Tell me something I don't already know." Sunny snorted in disgust. "I have the perfect outfit and no date. And despite my previous statements to the contrary, I do need an escort."

It was the first time she'd publicly admitted her deficiency. "But I'd have better luck finding gold at the end of a rainbow than digging up a suitable guy in Port Serenity."

"Ain't that the truth," Raylene agreed. "However, you cannot, repeat, *can not* go to that shindig without a man. Not when that mama's boy Walter Harrington is going to be the best man. We want him to rue the day he didn't stand up to that she-witch he calls a mother. It's called a woman's revenge. So, I have an idea."

God spare her from Raylene's ideas, especially if, as she suspected, it had something to do with Landry

Valliere.

"We'll go back to Plan A, not that we have a Plan B."

Sunny was tired. Her feet hurt. Her head was pounding, and she really wasn't in the mood for one of Raylene's nutty schemes. Too bad she couldn't seem to control her mouth.

"Remind me what Plan A is."

Raylene was wearing a leer that didn't bode well for Sunny's frame of mind. "Plan A is Landry. If you remember, that's how this whole thing got started. We saw him outside the window and discussed hiring him to take you to the wedding."

"No way."

"Oh, yes," Toolie squealed. "He's gorgeous, charming, and all the women love him."

"No."

"The jeans and T-shirt won't hack it, but we can get him all dressed up." By that time, Raylene was well into her *I'll take charge mode* and Toolie wasn't far behind.

"I said no." Talk about spitting in the wind.

"Tommy works at the Haberdashery, and I've got enough on him that he'll do anything I want."

Tommy was Raylene's second husband, or was he her third? Not that it mattered. At any rate the Haberdashery was Port Serenity's version of an emporium of fine gentlemen's clothing.

"So?" Why couldn't Sunny formulate a cogent sentence?

"So, we'll get Tommy to fix him up. I'm sure he can find something appropriate for us to 'borrow.'"

Raylene scrunched her fingers and made quotation marks in the air. "And I personally think Mr. Sexy will clean up just fine."

So did Sunny, and therein was the problem. He was heart stopping in a pair of old jeans and a T-shirt. What would he look like in a fancy suit? The image was enough to send her into a hot flash, and Lord in heaven, she was way too young for that kind of nonsense.

Even during his worst day at court, Landry had never experienced anything quite like his day at Double Date—pandemonium, potential hearing loss, and last, but certainly not least, estrogen overload.

Landry needed a cold brew and he was about to satisfy that desire when someone banged on his door. Considering he only knew four people in town, he was fairly sure he could identify his visitors, or visitor. If bad fortune hadn't been following him like a stray dog, he might get lucky and discover a cute little Texas rose on the other side of the door.

But the chances of that were slim and none. She scowled at him time every time she saw him. He opened the door to admit Toolie, Raylene, Penny and an obviously reluctant Sunny.

"Hey, ladies, come on in." Was his luck about to change?

Raylene, Toolie and Penny pranced in, claiming seats on the ratty couch. Sunny followed them and proceeded to prowl around the room.

Raylene was the first to speak. "We have a deal for you."

"A deal?" Landry asked, turning a wooden

kitchen chair around to straddle it.

The conspirators on the couch leaned forward in unison.

"It's a great opportunity." This time Toolie started the conversation.

"Sunny would like to give you a raise in return for an itsy, bitsy favor," she continued.

"Is that right?" Landry glanced at the woman in question. She looked like she'd rather smooch a boa constrictor than continue the discussion.

Landry didn't think of himself as a perverse kind of guy, but this time he couldn't resist teasing her.

"Miss Sunny, what kind of itsy, bitsy favor would you like from me?" Itsy, bitsy? He hadn't heard that term in ages and he was positive he'd never used it.

Sunny ran her hand through her hair. "I, uh, I, hmm…"

"Spit it out, girl," Raylene demanded.

"I need a date for Saturday."

She said it so fast Landry wasn't sure he'd heard her right.

"You want me to take you somewhere?"

Sunny heaved a deep sigh and plunked herself on the other end of the sofa. "Yes."

This was entertaining. Why would someone as attractive as Sunny have to hire a date?

As Landry watched emotions flit across her face, he contemplated his current life in the slow lane. Especially high on his "think about" list was his delectable boss and the stupid bet he'd made with Colby.

But first things first, and the initial item on the

agenda was Sunny McAllister—feisty, funny, blond, and extremely attractive. The problem was she wasn't his type. His style ran toward someone who was professional, cool and elegant; not a woman who elicited thoughts of baby car seats and big shaggy dogs. And did he mention vivid images of hot, sweaty sex.

Wait a minute. She said date, not marriage.

Sunny was praying that the floor would open up and swallow her. In the annals of embarrassing moments, this one had to be a new low. Not only was it humiliating, it was downright tacky. It took a few seconds to coordinate her mouth and brain, but she finally managed to take over the explanation.

"It's like this." That's the way she started her description of the wedding, her relationship with Walter and her current conundrum.

Chapter 10

The guy was unbelievable in a pair of faded jeans, but holy catfish, that hadn't prepared her for the sight of Landry in an expensive suit and a crisp white shirt. It didn't take more than three seconds for Sunny's initial rush of erotic thoughts to be diluted by Tommy's clucky, mother-hen routine.

"Don't spill anything on the suit that I can't get out by dry cleaning," Raylene's ex demanded as he nitpicked Landry's entire ensemble.

"Okay, sure. And don't wipe my face with the tie, right?"

Landry's reply was sarcasm at its best. Sunny was surprised he hadn't smacked the nervous haberdasher upside the head with the tie.

"You kids have fun," Raylene said, shooing them out the door.

"You're not my mother and this isn't the prom," Sunny snapped. She couldn't help herself. Sometimes her friend was simply too much to take. She wouldn't even be going to this wedding if the bride wasn't Uncle Dave's second cousin twice removed. And skipping a family shindig simply wasn't done.

"Here." Sunny threw her car keys to Landry. "You do have a driver's license, don't you?" She hated being a shrew, but this scenario was bringing out the worst in her.

"Yes, ma'am," her date replied, gracing her with a smile that could melt the hardest heart, and hers wasn't

made of tempered steel. Not by a long shot.

The ceremony was short, but Sunny was afraid the reception would be interminable. The Port Serenity Country Club was awash in a sea of white satin, pastel roses and twinkle lights. If her stomach hadn't felt as if it were being assaulted by an army of gastric gnomes, Sunny would have thought the place was a fairyland. In reality—especially considering her ex was flirting with some nubile debutante that even his mother could love—Sunny felt as if she were entering a prelude to purgatory.

"Would you like a drink?" Landry asked.

Not only did he clean up like a champ, he had the manners of a gentleman. And that led to more suspicion about his background and motivation. He was no more a drifter than Sunny was a pole dancer.

"Champagne?" Landry retrieved two flutes from the tray of a passing waiter. He was obviously used to taking charge. Could he be a CIA spy? Darn, she was getting nutty again.

"I'll bet we could find a strawberry or two if we looked around," he murmured, leaning over to nuzzle her neck.

Had they turned the air conditioner off, or was it just her? Sunny thought about ditching the jacket to her perfect outfit, but that would ruin the look she'd worked so hard to achieve.

Why *had* she spent so much time shopping? Oh, right. She wanted to impress Walter. And why did she want to do that?

She surreptitiously studied her ex-husband and tried to remember what it was that she had thought was attractive about him in the first place. Time had taken its toll. Beside the fact he was about as deep as kiddie wading pool, he was also going to seed. Even though they lived in the same town Sunny made sure they rarely ran into each other. So when she did see him she was always surprised at his appearance.

"Did I tell you how beautiful you look?" Landry's softly asked question jerked her out of her reverie. The intimate male voice sent goose bumps up and down Sunny's spine. Holy Batman!

Anna Belle and Eugenie had served up good manners with Sunny's Frosted Flakes, so it was time to drag them out, dust them off, and use them. "Thank you, that was very kind."

"Kindness has nothing to do with it," he murmured, placing his hand at the small of her back. "Would you like to wander over to the buffet and then find a table?"

Food, table—yep, that would work. "Sure. In fact, I see my cousin Liza over there. Let's join her." Sunny wasn't quite sure how Liza and Lily would react to her date; however, she knew she was about to find out. Her two favorite relatives rarely ever reserved judgement.

"Hey Liza, are you saving those seats?" Sunny asked. Her cousin responded by pulling her into a hug.

"Just for you and…" Liza waved a hand in Landry's direction, giving him a thorough survey in the process. "Lily and I have been looking everywhere for

you."

"This is my date, Landry Valliere. Landry, this is

my cousin Liza Henderson and her friend Charlie Taylor." Liza was a widow. Charlie was her business partner and one of her best buddies.

The two men shook hands and when Liza extended hers in greeting, Landry made the surprise move of kissing it instead.

Sunny wasn't sure what that was all about, but the look on her cousin's face was priceless. It wasn't often Liza was rendered speechless

"Sweetie, who *is* this marvelous specimen?" That honeyed drawl could belong only to her other cousin, Lily.

As Sunny made the appropriate introductions, she surreptitiously checked out the table settings. Big problem. There were forks of every shape, size and description. She was an honors graduate from Miss Alicia's School of Etiquette, and she didn't recognize half of the utensils.

She really didn't want Landry to be embarrassed. Maybe she could give him a few subtle hints. Her misgivings, however, were totally unfounded.

Who *was* he?

"What did you say you do for a living?" That question came from Lily's husband, Clayton, otherwise known as Clay. Sunny couldn't wait to hear the answer.

"I'm having a sort of temporary career change," Landry answered.

Obviously not satisfied with that information, Clay persevered. "From what to what?"

Sunny's family was very protective. Sometimes that proved to be useful. At other times, it was simply aggravating.

"I work for Sunny right now. When I return to New Orleans, I'll go back to a little business my partner and I have."

Sunny hoped to goodness that "little business" didn't involve the wrong side of the law.

"What kind of business?" Clay persisted. Everyone at the table waited intently for Landry's answer.

"I deal with the criminal justice system."

Sunny's heart took a nosedive. She was right; he *was* too good to be true. He was gorgeous, funny, brave, and probably wanted by the law.

Damn it!

The interrogation was cut short when Holly Horatio—Viola's only heir and a bimbo extraordinaire—barreled up. The fact she was missing a few brain cells was negated by the small detail that she had a body reminiscent of Marilyn Monroe. And even more unfortunate, she was accompanied by Walter.

"Well, hello there," Holly gushed, practically pushing Sunny out of the way. "Mother told me all about you," she said to Landry. "I would have welcomed you sooner but I don't get my hair done *here*. I go to Houston. Do you like it?" she asked, suggestively weaving her fingers through her highlighted locks.

Sunny had no doubt Holly had paid a fortune for that over-processed mess. She was so busy thinking catty thoughts that she forgot Walter was standing beside her.

When he spoke to Liza, Sunny suddenly had the epiphany that her ex had always blended into the woodwork, and that even without his mother's interference, they never would have stayed together.

Walter's personality was eclipsed by his strong-willed mother, while Sunny yearned for someone who made her skin tingle and her heart palpitate. That certainly didn't describe Walter. It was sad but true; theirs hadn't been a match made in heaven.

"Hello, Sunny." Walter finally acknowledged her presence. "You look nice," he said.

Nice! Nice! She'd worked damned hard to make him lament the day he'd dumped her, and all he said was she looked *nice*. What had happened to the stab of lust, or at the very least the drool she'd hoped to achieve? Defeat had such a sour taste.

"Are you all right," Landry asked, putting his arm around her waist.

"I'm fine," Sunny assured him, hoping against hope that he'd drop the subject. She really didn't want to discuss her marriage, or Walter, or anything else that was vaguely personal.

Bless her heart, Holly demanded his attention. "So, Mother said she baked a batch of brownies for you, seeing as how you were so courageous, and all. My mother makes the best brownies in town. Don't ya think?"

Landry's expression didn't reveal a thing. Was he buying into the bimbo's spiel or not?

"Let's dance." Holly practically yanked him out of his chair.

"Don't worry," Liza remarked as Holly steamrolled Landry toward the dance floor. "I don't know the guy. But I'm sure he has more sense than to be taken in by that tart."

Charlie and Clay chuckled. And as a result of that

their nonverbal contribution to the conversation, Lily admonished her hubby. "Watch yourself."

"Yes, sweetie," Clay replied. Then both men laughed again.

"I'm gonna invite Mr. Valliere to Sunday dinner. That will give us a chance to grill him properly," Liza announced. Her sister nodded in agreement. They might not look alike, but sometimes it seemed like they worked with a single mind.

"No, you're not," Sunny exclaimed. "He doesn't mean anything to me, so why would you want to ask him over. That seems so...so intimate, especially considering he's a stranger. I've only known him two weeks."

"That's precisely why we're having him to dinner. If he plans to hang out with our favorite relative, we want to get the straight skinny on him."

Just butter her butt and call her a biscuit.

Chapter 11

True to their word, Liza and Lily issued an invitation that Landry couldn't resist. So there they were, one big happy family doing Sunday dinner. Au contraire! It was more like the Spanish Inquisition than a friendly meal.

And astonishing as it might seem, the family had lost almost all the battles in this war of wills. Landry had more moves than Tom Brady.

"Is this anything like your mama's fried chicken recipe?" Anna Belle asked.

She was good. No wonder—her skills had been honed from years of dealing with fifth graders.

"No, ma'am. My mother never was much of a cook. But this is wonderful. My compliments to the chef," he said with a grin.

Sunny had to admit that he knew the perfect path to a Texas woman's heart.

Landry Valliere was as slick as greased owl spit—much too smooth for Sunny's taste.

Yeah right!

She watched in awe as both Cora, their long time housekeeper, and Anna Belle turned pink. Cora had to be at least eighty but she still knew her way around a kitchen, and apparently she wasn't immune to a compliment.

And Anna Belle—what could you say about Anna Belle Carpenter Nunn, other than she was a firecracker. After she retired from teaching, she went straight into activism and then segued to politics and the city council.

"Have you decided whether you're going to run for mayor?" Sunny asked. She had a few tricks up her sleeve, and engaging Anna Belle, Eugenie and Sheriff Dave in a discussion of local government was the easiest way she knew of to change the subject. Landry obviously realized what she was doing and sent her a smile of gratitude.

Her little trick, however, didn't deter her determined cousins.

"So, did I hear you say you were from New Orleans? I had a sorority sister from Slidell. Is that anywhere near your home?" Lily asked.

Sunny whacked her on the shin; however, it didn't stop her for more than a second. She was a woman on a mission.

Landry gave her one of the smiles that Sunny was starting to think of as his cat-in-the-creamery grins.

"I grew up in the French Quarter," he replied. "But, I don't live there now."

"Where *do* you live now?" Clay asked. Lily had unobtrusively lobbed the conversational ball to her husband.

There was the grin again. "I live here."

In a skirmish of wits, Landry had to be declared the winner.

Clay had the good grace to laugh. "I know when I'm beat. So what do you think about those Cowboys? Think they can win the Super Bowl this year?"

Fortunately, Landry had a working knowledge of football; and no matter how hard the sisters' tried to derail the sports conversation, even *they* couldn't breach the brotherhood of the pigskin.

So Sunday dinner progressed. The cuisine was a surefire contender for the comfort food hall of fame.

"I hope you left room for some peach cobbler and homemade ice cream." Anna Belle stood to collect the dishes.

"Give me about thirty minutes and I'll be ready," Landry said with a laugh. "Why don't you sit down and let us clean up." He took the stack of plates out of her hand.

If he kept that up, her family would adopt him, and that would make him her brother. Aargh!

Landry suppressed a grin. Sunny's relatives were not only delightful; they were nosy as all get-out. Although he didn't know them well, he suspected Liza and Lily wouldn't go down without a fight, and if he wasn't careful, they would eventually manage to trip him up.

"That was delicious," Landry declared, barely resisting the urge to rub his stomach. After the younger members of the family cleaned the kitchen, they adjourned to the sunporch for coffee and sweets.

It didn't take a rocket scientist to realize that the minute the cobbler was put away, the questions would recommence. Fortunately, Sunny had another plan.

"I understand the mayor was caught crawling around under Miss Dolly's shrubbery," she commented, almost too casually.

He could tell by her subtle smirk that she knew exactly what she was doing. She was so cute he couldn't resist giving her hand a gentle squeeze.

Sheriff Dave choked on his coffee, and Anna

Belle gave an unladylike guffaw.

"That twit can't keep his zipper up. He thinks every woman in town has the hots for him. Delusional old goat." Lily wasn't at all reticent about describing the politician's proclivities.

Smart guy that he was, Dave nodded, but remained silent.

Anna Belle didn't feel compelled to follow suit. "Miss Dolly wouldn't spit on the geezer if he was on fire."

In the ensuing discussion Landry discovered that Miss Dolly was the estranged wife of Harold Trout, the president of the city council. And the police had been involved in several skirmishes involving the trio. Writers for the soap operas writers would have a field day with this one.

"I talked to him after my deputy found him with mud all over his knees. He claims he was looking for his dog." Dave laughed as he joined the discussion. "The problem is he doesn't have a pooch. Even dogs can't stand him."

"The rumor is that Harold cornered the old fool at the Kiwanis meeting and threatened to beat the stuffin' out of him if he didn't straighten up and fly right." Anna Belle gave a huff and settled back on the wicker settee. "If the mayor doesn't watch out, I'm gonna help Harold." She negated her threat with a giggle.

"However, I plan to be a bit more devious. I'm going to personally make sure he gets voted out of office," she admitted.

"I heard at the salon that Harold's taken to packing a gun," Sunny said, then leaned back to wait for the blowup.

"Lord have mercy!" Eugenie exclaimed. "Those two old men are as blind as bats. We can't have someone getting shot at a city council meeting. What can you do about it, Dave?"

"I really don't want to hear any of this," the sheriff said, scratching his head. Then he sighed in resignation. "I'll send a deputy to the next meeting. Do you think that'll help?" He addressed his question to Anna Belle.

"I sure hope so. We haven't had a murder in Port Serenity in quite a while, at least not since we had all those dead bodies floating up on the beach. We don't want one now, especially not if it involves a couple of our esteemed city fathers."

Dead bodies floating up on the beach? That sounded more like Houston than Port Serenity. Perhaps taking some time away from murder and mayhem *would* be good for his soul. But anything permanent would put a huge crimp in his income, and leaving his practice would be a gigantic lifestyle change. Where had *that* idea come from? He would *never* consider doing anything that drastic. Or would he?

As much as he hated to admit it, the relaxed atmosphere of Port Serenity was appealing—as long as there weren't any bodies on the beach.

Chapter 12

Sunny was enjoying a Monday morning coffee with Liza when her cousin tossed in a conversational grenade. "A thank-you note? Landry sat down and wrote Anna Belle a note, on paper, with a pen? And he delivered it." That did it—the guy was definitely not homeless, nor was he down on his luck. So exactly what was he doing in Port Serenity? And why had he been holding her hand at dinner? Not that she minded. No indeedy!

"Yes, ma'am. And just to throw in my two cents' worth, I think he's a mighty handsome man," Liza announced.

So did Sunny, but she wasn't about to admit that to her cousin. There wasn't a man alive she'd let under her skin, even if he was the most appealing person she'd ever known. It was that once-burned twice-shy stuff.

"You invited me to coffee so you could tell me Landry has manners?"

"No, you dummy. Lily and I want you to know we're giving him our seal of approval. We're not sure about his employment situation but we think he has potential."

The next day Sunny was still pondering the Landry situation, when the object of her ruminations strolled in the back door. The salon was closed on Mondays so she hadn't seen him since their infamous Sunday dinner.

She couldn't decide whether to play it cool or be totally mortified. Unfortunately, her family hadn't been very subtle in their questioning, and they'd been even less circumspect in bestowing their endorsement.

Darn their hides.

All things considered—pushy relatives, resorting to hiring a date, etcetera, etcetera—he must think she was the biggest wallflower in Texas. And considering the fact her love life was virtually nonexistent, she probably was. The pity party had to stop. Right this minute!

He was handsome, fun, and apparently had a working knowledge of Miss Manners. Add it all up, and her renegade heart lapsed into wishful thinking. That had to come to an end as well.

Something wasn't quite right about him; and as hard as she tried, Sunny couldn't figure out what it was. One thing for certain; he was as out of his element in a beauty salon as an English teacher at a rap concert.

Sunny's family was a hoot, and Liza and Lily had missed their calling. Their interrogation skills would put the CIA to shame. Even the wedding had been entertaining and Landry wasn't a big fan of nuptials. It seemed like saying "I do" was a prelude to disaster. Or, was that just the cynic in him talking.

Maybe his life in the fast lane wasn't all it was cracked up to be. In a rare moment of doubt, Landry had second thoughts about his chosen lifestyle. Would it be feasible to live and work somewhere other than the Big Easy?

Hi knee jerk reaction was no. But why not? That was a question he couldn't answer.

"Hey, Mr. Landry. How 'ya doin'?" The friendly greeting came from Sunny's janitor, Bubba Gene Guthrie.

"Not bad, Bubba Gene, not bad at all."

"I love playing with the dogs that Miss Penny washes. Don't you?"

"I like dogs, Bubba Gene. They know when someone's a good guy."

Bubba Gene broke into a huge grin. "That they do, Mr. Landry. That they do."

Shortly after Landry started work at Double Date, Raylene had told him the story about Bubba Gene and Sunny's campaign to help him become a functioning member of society.

The gentle giant, with the IQ of a small child, had lived with his mother his entire life. When Mrs. Guthrie died, he'd been set adrift. That is, until Sunny gave him a job at the salon. Not only did she trust Bubba Gene to work as her janitor, she'd cajoled, bribed and charmed several friends into hiring him as their gardener. And if adoring looks were any indication, Bubba Gene would do anything for his boss and friend.

"Did you have a nice weekend," Landry asked.

"Yes, sir, I shor' did. That movie I'm partial to was at the Grand on Saturday." He hitched up his overalls and scratched his belly. "You know the one with uh….uh…Raylene, what's her name?"

Raylene was preparing her station for the upcoming day. "Elsa," she replied without looking up. "He's talking about *Frozen,* " she explained to Landry.

Landry nodded, understanding everything. "Oh, okay. Hey, Bubba, I'm glad you enjoyed yourself."

"Yes, sir. I even had enough money to buy popcorn," Bubba Gene said as he continued to sweep, humming as he worked.

Landry watched the janitor for a few moments. In Port Serenity it was possible to be happy with few material possessions. In his world, a guy could get killed for his sneakers.

Perhaps there was something to be said for the slow and easy way of life; not that he was really considering staying. Or to paraphrase Bubba Gene, "No, siree."

Landry had barely wiped the grin from his face when his incredibly attractive boss stomped toward the back of the salon.

Yep, she stomped. Or at least she made as much racket as someone who didn't weigh more a hundred pounds soakin' wet could make. Oops! Did he really drop that g? And was that speech pattern catching?

"Here." She poked a plate at him, forcing him to bend over to prevent being maimed.

"What's this?" he asked, holding up a platter of baked goods.

"It's a coconut cake. Holly Horatio left it for you. Eat it quick or we'll get ants, and I don't want to have to call the exterminator," she announced before marching off.

"Our boss lady doesn't look like too happy," Raylene said, grinning ear to ear as she continued to get ready for her onslaught of clients.

He tried to hand her the cake. "Would you like this?"

"Not me. I don't like coconut."

74

Landry suspected it was more like she didn't like Holly Horatio, but he kept his mouth shut. He was a smart guy, and he had an Ivy League education to prove it.

"I'll take it," Bubba Gene said, leaning on his broom. "Mama used to make me those. She's gone now, ya know."

Landry didn't know how to respond so he simply handed over the cake.

Bubba Gene wandered off with a smile plastered on his face.

"You made his day, ya' know that? I just hope Holly didn't mix up the salt and sugar. She's not exactly the brightest gal around."

Landry had already figured that out so he didn't bother to answer.

"Uh-oh. Here comes another one of your admirers." Raylene nodded in the direction of the front desk. "And it looks like she's bearing gifts."

Landry barely managed to keep a straight face as a slightly chubby woman carrying a plate of cookies barreled his way. She would have been attractive, if her hair hadn't been a weird shade of olive green.

Landry looked to Toolie for guidance; this was her client, but she grinned and continued to putter around her station.

Prior to his gig at Double Date, Landry's only experience with beauty salons had been periodic haircut appointments. After two weeks at the salon, he had a new appreciation for the profession. They heard more sob stories than a bartender.

"Here you go." The woman shoved the

improvised tin-foil plate at him. "Cookies. Peanut butter. I hope you're not allergic to peanuts. You should call my niece. She plays the piano." The woman didn't wait for him to reply before she picked up a strand of hair and waved it at Toolie.

"Toolie, you've got to help me," she wailed.

No kidding!

"Landry, would you please give Charlene a nice relaxing shampoo." Toolie ended her request with an expression that could only be interpreted as a cross between a smirk and a wink.

"Charlene, sweetie, you pop yourself right over to the shampoo bowl. Landry will take care of you. And why don't you tell him how you got yourself into that fix?"

Landry ushered the distraught woman over to the sink and managed to get her settled before she started her story.

"I have an invitation to this great wedding next weekend. The reception is going to be at the Houston Country Club," she gushed. "Can you believe it? My cousin's cousin is taking me as his date. So, naturally, I wanted to look my best. And I was getting some grey so I did the color myself. I don't know what happened. I hope to goodness Toolie can fix it."

So did Landry, but he was too smart to voice his misgivings. That was just the beginning of the woman's chatter. It was enough to drive a sane man crazy.

The next client was a brunette he hadn't met before. She was prim, proper and so uptight she looked like she was about to snap. Something about her reminded Landry of many of the teachers he'd had in high school.

But the good news was she didn't look like she'd ever baked a cookie.

His illusion of safety evaporated like mist on a hot day when he glanced at Raylene. She was laughing her head off—obviously at his expense.

What now?

It didn't take Landry long to figure it out. The brunette *really* enjoyed a good shampoo. The more Landry massaged her scalp, the louder she got.

"Ooh, ooh, aaah. Oh, yes."

"You are dead meat," he mouthed to Raylene. The twit responded with a belly laugh.

That was only the beginning of the day. They had a parade of senior citizens sporting corkscrew purple perms, housewives who thought they needed a trim and a couple of teenagers who wanted purple hair. The seniors and housewives were not only bearing goodies for Landry, they were also armed with names and phone numbers of cousins, aunts, friends and one woman even brought the number of a checker from the Piggly Wiggly. The front counter looked like a bake sale at the Baptist church.

The last client was paying her bill when Landry adjourned to the back of the salon. He'd seen enough hair to last him a lifetime, and he'd had his butt grabbed more than once.

"I have to apologize," Sunny said. He hadn't heard her come in, but there she was in all her pixie glory. She'd had a hard day and she was still as cute and luscious as a Hill Country peach.

Funny thing, he'd never had libidinous thoughts

about cute before. His previous women had all been glamorous. In fact, he'd never harbored ideas of a permanent life before, and with this woman, that's all he seemed to be contemplating. *That* had to come to a halt. Immediately, if not sooner!

Landry's only goal was to win the bet and then get back to his law practice, post haste. When in doubt he always went with the old saying, better the devil you know. And this Texas "devil" was a total enigma. Not that he thought Sunny was evil—no indeed! And therein was the problem.

"What are you apologizing for, peaches?"

"For that whole coconut cake debacle." She waved a hand in the air, somehow managing to look chagrined and sly at the same time. It was a cool trick if you could pull it off—and she managed. "Did you call me peaches?"

"No apology necessary, and yes, I did," Landry admitted with a grin. He wondered if her pique was motivated by jealousy. Holly Horatio, Sophia Vergara—yep, he strongly suspected Sunny had met the green-eyed monster. She liked him. Hot damn!

"I'm starving. Could I talk you into going to dinner with me?" he asked.

Sunny perused the array of baked goods before she raised an eyebrow.

"I need something containing protein," he said.

"Right. I can't believe I'm saying this, but I am tired of banana nut bread. If this silly baking contest continues much longer, I'm gonna weigh three hundred pounds. Lord in heaven, the women in this town are acting like twits. You'd think they'd never seen a good-looking guy before."

"Good-looking, huh." Landry couldn't resist another grin.

"Don't let it go to your head. Most of them watch pro wrestling."

"Don't knock it. The WWF guys are ripped."

Sunny gave him one of her "whatever" looks and changed the subject. "What did you think of Cora Rutherford?"

Although Landry was normally good with names, the clients at Double Date were getting all mixed up.

"You'll have to remind me which one she was."

"She's the brunette who equates a shampoo with, uh…" Sunny broke into a huge laugh but eventually managed to finish her description. "Let's just say it's a little more intense for her than most people."

"Oh, yeah. She'd be hard to forget. Does that kind of thing happen often?" God he hoped not!

Chapter 13

The Port Serenity Café was known throughout the county for its gut-busting chili dogs (with onions and cheese), greasy cheeseburgers and calorie-laden milkshakes. The dinner fare was cholesterol at its best, and Landry loved it. New Orleans dining was internationally acclaimed. But sometimes in fray of everyday life, he forgot that gourmet was not the norm across a great portion of the country.

"Did you like your dinner?" Sunny gave his clean plate a significant look. "What have you been eating lately?"

Landry hated to admit his diet had leaned heavily toward peanut butter sandwiches, Cheerios and cheap beer—with an occasional bologna sandwich thrown in for variety. "Not much good stuff. Dinner was delicious. Would you like some dessert?"

"No, I don't think so. If you get a hankering for some sweets just go back to the salon and take whatever you want. Please, take it all. I don't need the calories. Although his apartment key worked on both doors, Landry wasn't comfortable wandering around the salon after hours.

"I've been promoted, haven't I?"

"Yes," she said with a smile.

"Cool. I'm stuffed. Can I talk you into going for a walk?"

"Uh-huh. A walk sounds good. I love summer evenings. That's when the wind dies and it gets cool. All the little critters come out to play."

Landry had never actually pondered the nightlife

of small animals, and calling the temperature cool was a bit of an overstatement.

It seemed natural for Landry to take her hand as they strolled down the boulevard. The fragrant scent of honeysuckle tickled Sunny's nose, bringing back wonderful memories of her childhood. Cicadas chirped their delight that the day had turned into evening. The old-fashioned lamps illuminated the sidewalk, giving the street the feeling of another time and place.

In Port Serenity, the period between dusk and dark was the time when children played hide-and-seek and collected fireflies to be kept overnight in a Mason jar. Although life had changed considerably in the past twenty years, there were some traditions, especially in a small Texas town, that remained static. It all led to a feeling of permanence.

Adding to her enjoyment of the evening was the fact she was holding hands with a handsome man who seemed to want nothing more than her company. That hadn't been the case with Walter.

Stop that! Sunny mentally excised all thoughts of her ex-husband. He was part of her past, not her present.

"Who's this?" Landry asked as he pulled her to a stop in front of the statue of a man on a horse.

"That's the first Texas Ranger. I can't remember his name, but he's famous. I suspect he was a badass."

"Cool."

"Yeah, well."

Landry chuckled, and then sat down on the concrete bench. He took her hand, silently urging her to join him.

"Let's talk."

Under ordinary circumstances, Sunny would have been tempted to break into chuckles. Imagine that—a man who wanted to talk. It was especially interesting considering that this one harbored more secrets than the NSA.

"Okay," she agreed, joining him on the bench. Curiosity overrode her protective instinct.

"This is nice," he murmured, leaning back.

"Yes, it is, isn't it?" She was about to get comfortable when he threw her a curve ball

"Why don't you tell me about your ex-husband?"

"My what?"

"Your ex. I've been wondering about him ever since the wedding. Being around him upsets you, doesn't it?"

Sunny briefly pondered the question and then decided to reply. Considering she'd bribed Landry into accompanying her to the wedding, she owed him an explanation.

"His name is Walter, but you know that. He's not one of my favorite people."

"That was loud and clear."

"Did I tell you I used to be a schoolteacher?"

"No, you didn't." Landry sat up as if he was really interested in the rest of the story.

"Yep, I was an English teacher. After I graduated from the University of Texas I came home and immediately got a job at the high school. The fact that they hired me after a ten-minute interview should have been a huge red flag, or an omen of things to come." Sunny started to shrug, but ended up grinning. "His

82

mother was on the school board. I needed a job. I had a brand new degree and I was thrilled." She did another "whatever" motion with her hands.

"Walter was working at his mother's real estate office. We met at church and fell in love." Sunny verbally emphasized the *L* word. "At least I thought we were in love. In reality, he was in lust and I was simply stupid."

"That sounds familiar. I have several divorced friends."

"We were happy for all of about, oh say, thirty-three seconds. Walter is a mama's boy.' Are you familiar with that interesting character flaw?"

"Not really."

"Let me tell you, it's a killer in a marriage. His mother had access to our checking account even after we were married." Sunny shook her head. "She had a key to our house and would come over at all hours of the day and night. But the worst thing was she started following me. And Walter didn't do squat. She'd say 'jump', and he'd reply 'how high?' However, I probably would have stayed married to him if he hadn't issued an ultimatum."

"He had the guts to give you an ultimatum?"

"Oh, yeah. After a couple of years teaching and dealing with Beatrice Harrington, I knew that our marriage wasn't destined to last." Sunny chuckled. "I mentally called her Beatrice the Beast. Guess that didn't help, huh? Anyway, the salon came on the market so I took money from my small trust fund and put a down payment on the business. Then, I quit my teaching job and went to cosmetology school. I knew I'd make more owning the salon than I could as a teacher. Plus, I'd finally realized that teaching wasn't what I wanted to do."

"And?"

"Walter's mother didn't think it was acceptable to have a beautician for a daughter-in-law, so he told me he'd divorce me if I didn't ditch my stupid idea. Dear old mom never thought I was good enough for her baby boy, especially since I started life in a trailer park. To put it mildly, snobbery was her strong suit."

"That's tough, especially in a town this small."

"It certainly was. The ironic thing is I suspect Walter will eventually try to get out from under her wing. And when he does, I'm afraid he's going to do something stupid. It's not that I dislike him as much as I feel sorry for him."

Landry responded with a shrug.

"So turnabout is fair play. How about you?" Sunny smiled at him.

"How about *me* what?"

"Do you have a wife, a girlfriend, a whatever?"

"I've never been married, and as far as girlfriends go, yeah, there have been some."

"Any serious ones?"

"You certainly are nosy." Landry tempered his comment with a grin.

"What can I say," Sunny agreed. "I told you everything about my Walter experience, pitiful as it was. Now it's your turn."

Landry casually put his arm on the bench behind her. "A while back I decided it was time to settle down, so I started dating a woman named Amelie. Looking back, I suppose I picked her because our families have been friends for years and it seemed like an easy solution. That was a huge mistake. She got so clingy she was smothering."

"She sounds like kudzu."

Landry grinned at her analogy. "Yeah, like kudzu. At any rate, I'm afraid I didn't a very good job of breaking up because she calls me periodically or drops by my house uninvited."

Okay, maybe he was running from a bad girlfriend. That would be better than fleeing the law.

Then Sunny's curiosity got the best of her good manners. "Is she pretty?"

"Do you mean Amelie?" Landry asked.

Sunny nodded, feeling like a jealous nitwit. What did she have to feel jealous about?

"Yes, she's pretty," Landry said, running his finger down her cheek. "And that's enough discussion of Amelie. Tell me about Sunny McAllister's life."

Sunny then told him the story of her mother's death and the Carpenter sisters adopting her.

Landry didn't say a word, so Sunny continued. "I have one last comment about Walter. Neither he nor his mother intended to do anything nice for me, but in reality they did me the biggest favor in the world. They rocked me out of my complacency, and voila, I'm now the ex- Mrs. Walter Harrington and loving it. I consider my success a sweet revenge."

Landry understood the concept of revenge. In his profession, he saw it every day. However, in his experience it usually included the use of a .357 Magnum. Things were certainly different in Port Serenity.

85

He was about to kiss her. And kiss her. And kiss her. And if there was a God in the heavens, Sunny would reciprocate.

He's gonna kiss me. Oh, my word, he's gonna kiss me. That was Sunny's last rational thought before Landry pulled her into his arms and touched his lips to hers. Their first kiss started out gently. It was perfect for a night bathed in the glow of moonlight. It took him mere minutes to elevate the exploration of her mouth from innocent to sensuous.

Ooh la, la.

Sunny barely had time for her brain to process the signals her nerve endings were sending, before he pulled back and rested his forehead on hers.

"That was, uh, that was great."

Was it ever!

"I think I should walk you home now."

That was *not* what she wanted to hear.

"Uh, okay." On a scale of one to ten, Sunny's enthusiasm for strolling home rated somewhere close to a one-minus. More kissing—that rated an eight or nine—never mind they were in a public place.

"I live a couple of blocks in that direction." She indicated a tree lined street leading away from the main street.

Much to Sunny's delight, Landry pulled her to her feet and drew her into his arms. But best of all, he planted little butterfly kisses all over her face and neck.

Merciful heavens!

Chapter 14

The next morning, Landry was still reeling from the Sunny encounter that his libido had labeled THE KISS. He was definitely thinking in capital letters, and *that* made him extremely nervous.

Landry's face had been on the cover of several magazines as one of New Orleans' most eligible bachelors. He'd also had more than his share of girlfriends; women whose attributes spanned the spectrum from gorgeous bodies, to highly-educated minds, to vibrant personalities. Just thinking about Sunny conjured visions of a white bungalow with green shutters, a porch swing and a calico cat.

Whoa! That was an exact description of her house. The thought slammed him back into reality. Even if he could fit into her life, would she be able to forgive his duplicity? Hell, no! She was a firecracker and he was nothing but a con man and a liar. And the whole situation had come about because of a stupid bet.

So how was he going to dig himself out of the self-imposed hole? Landry was contemplating the situation when Toolie groaned.

"Anything I can help you with?" He thought he'd make the offer even though he barely knew the difference between henna and a highlight.

"No, Winnie Thompson wants me to redo her perm. She claims it's not tight enough. Merciful Pete, that hair of hers is tighter than poodle curls. She constantly wants a redo for something or the other."

Toolie slammed the appointment book shut and marched

over to prepare for her customers, including the infamous Winnie Thompson.

So far, Sunny hadn't appeared. That was unusual since she normally opened the shop. Not that Landry was getting worried, but it wasn't like her to be late.

"Hey, Raylene. Does Sunny have any appointments this morning?"

"Not that I know of. But she always comes in." Raylene frowned. "I wonder where she is?"

That was a good question. But, Landry wasn't her boyfriend or her daddy, and definitely not her keeper. She certainly wasn't obliged to share her schedule with him.

In lieu of breakfast, Landry grabbed a fresh banana nut muffin. The flow of baked goods had abated, more than likely because he hadn't shown any interest in dipping into Port Serenity's dating pool.

After devouring the first ten or twelve dozen cookies, he'd decided the chocolate chip should be the state dessert of Texas. The small delicacies came in every shape, size and convolution—featuring chunks, chips, oatmeal, raisins, hunks of candy bars and even peanut butter, but shouldn't those be called peanut-butter cookies?

Landry was pondering the peanut thing almost as seriously as he would a tricky criminal defense. That's when realization hit him. It was time to ditch the bet, graciously set his partner up with his sister, and get the heck out of Port Serenity. If he didn't make an escape soon, his brain would curdle like buttermilk. Was there something in the water that was making him crazy?

The entire time he was shampooing Betty Sue

Hilliard, he was pondering the possibility of water pollution. Thank God, she was one of the quiet ones. He had just completed her final rinse when he heard a loud noise up front.

What now?

Unfortunately, this "what now" ended up being worse than all of the other events—including the overload of chocolate chip cookies and the aborted robbery.

"Raylene, what are we going to do?" Sunny was hysterically waving the portable phone.

Landry took the receiver out of her hands. "Sweetheart, what's wrong?" he asked, pulling her into his arms.

He didn't miss the look Raylene shot him. She'd caught the "sweetheart" remark but Sunny obviously hadn't. Her answer was to burrow her face in his T-shirt and let go with a fresh surge of tears.

An audience had gathered and Landry looked to the ladies for guidance. The unison of shrugs indicated he was on his own.

"Sunny, sweetheart. Look at me." He cupped her chin and lifted her face. "Tell me the problem. Maybe I can help."

She swiped at her face like a small child. "I don't think you can do anything. Not unless you're some kind of super lawyer."

That hit closer to home than he was willing to admit.

"What do you mean?"

"Bubba Gene's been arrested for murder."

The ladies reacted in unison.

"What?" Raylene squealed.

Landry felt his lawyer persona take over. Someone had to take charge and he couldn't help himself.

"Raylene, Toolie, why don't you take the ladies on back and finish whatever you were doing. Sunny and I are going over to the beach." He grabbed two Cokes from the cooler before guiding her out the door, narrowly avoiding two kids on skateboards.

"Let's sit in the shade and you can tell me all about it," Landry suggested. She remained uncharacteristically silent. He'd never seen Sunny without a comment on the tip of her tongue.

"Here," he said as he popped the top of the Coke can and handed it to her. "You need some sugar."

"You need some sugar?" Sunny barely suppressed a hysterical bout of giggles. Any Texas girl worth her margarita knew that "sugar" meant a kiss. And yes, sirree, she surely could use some sugar.

He poked the Coke at her again. Oh, right. He meant real sugar.

A sip of caffeine and sugar was all it took for Sunny to pull herself together, at least enough to respond to his questions.

"Teddy Errol Flynn called to tell me. We went to elementary school together and he's a deputy now. Sheriff Dave knew we were friends." Sunny sniffed before continuing.

"You know I got Bubba Gene some jobs mowing

lawns, right?"

Landry nodded.

"Anyway, Aunt Hallie Rule was one of those people. Anna Belle is her niece or something like that. She helped me talk Aunt Hallie into hiring Bubba. The woman's cranky and rich, and lives in this big old house on the edge of town. She was lonely, and Bubba's such a gentle soul. We all thought he'd be good for her. But, now she's dead, and her maid found Bubba Gene standing over her body with blood all over his hands," Sunny ended her explanation with a wail.

Well, damn!

Not only did Landry like Bubba Gene—who was obviously in big trouble—but this turn of events also meant the jig was up. Landry was about to have his identity revealed.

Bubba Gene couldn't be a killer; and Landry wasn't about to allow an innocent friend go down on a murder rap—at least not without a fight.

"Drink up, sweetheart, we'll go see the sheriff," he instructed.

Sunny gave him a glance filled with doubt, but in the end she complied. She probably didn't have a better idea.

Landry followed her into the basement of the courthouse where the Sheriff's office was located. Cop shops across the nation looked and smelled the same. Some entrepreneur had obviously cornered the market on metal desks, metal chairs and nondescript cubicle partitions. Then this unnamed person created a ubiquitous decorating scheme, cleverly know as bureaucratic BS. Add the sterile ambiance to the unmistakable aroma of stale coffee, musty paper and unwashed bodies, and Landry was transported back to a world he knew.

"Hey, Miss Sunny, I'll bet you're here to see the sheriff. He said you'd be round purty quick."

"Yes, sir." Sunny gave the wiry deputy a gracious smile. Her good manners were alive and well, so she must be feeling better. Although Landry suspected she'd use "yes, sir" and "yes, ma'am" even if she was in the throes of typhoid.

"He said to send you on back to his office. You know where it is."

"I sure do. Thanks, Jimmy. I appreciate it."

On the way to their destination, Sunny stopped at almost every cubicle for a quick howdy. Why did the fact she was on a first name basis with the entire police force disturb him? Could it be jealousy? No way, not Super Lawyer. Jealousy wasn't his style.

Landry was one of the best defense attorneys in the South and that's exactly the role he planned to resume. But how could he accomplish that objective without alienating Miss Sunny? Funny how he'd started thinking in terms of Miss this, and Miss that.

It was that Texas thing again.

He was formulating a plan when the sheriff wandered in, a cup of coffee in one hand, a pile of folders in the other.

"Hey, honey. How ya doin?" he asked before enveloping Sunny in a bear hug.

"Okay," she paused, "no, not really. Bubba

Gene's my friend."

"I know. Why don't you sit down and I'll tell you what I can."

When Sunny complied, he affectionately patted her on the head.

"He was found standing over Aunt Hallie's body with blood all over him. He's gonna need a hotshot lawyer, because— at least at first glance—it doesn't look good."

"Uncle Dave, he doesn't have any money. He lives on Social Security, what he makes at my place, and his gardening jobs. Believe me, that's not much. And we both know he has the IQ of a third grader. He couldn't have killed her."

"I know. Don't worry; the county has a public defender so he won't be without representation."

Sunny didn't bother to suppress her anguish. "Is Jimmy Arbuckle still the public defender?"

Dave nodded.

"That's freakin' fantastic. He cheated his way through high school. I'll bet dollars to doughnuts his law degree came out of a catalog."

"He really does have a law degree." Dave assured her.

"And I'll bet he was at the bottom of his class."

Dave didn't bother to dispute her claim.

"I want to help Bubba Gene but I don't have the money for high-dollar Houston shark."

Shark?

Despite her uncomplimentary assessment of his profession, Landry knew he was going to help Sunny and Bubba Gene. He just needed time to come up with a viable plan. One that would get Bubba Gene a "get out of jail free" card and still allow Landry time to convince Sunny he wasn't a lying jerk.

Chapter 14

It had required a tag team effort to convince Sunny to go home. In truth, Sheriff Dave's firm assertion that she wouldn't be any help, and that he wasn't about to let her see Bubba Gene in her current state of mind, was what finally sent her home. Otherwise, Landry suspected they'd still be at the courthouse instead of sitting on her porch swing.

"What can I do?" She had asked the question at least three times. "I don't think there's any way I can come up with the money we'll need to defend him properly."

Landry ran his fingers through her short spiky hair. "Let me ask you this. Why is it so important to you?"

She leaned forward, placing her elbows on her knees. "Years ago his mom was my Sunday school teacher. Then later she came into the salon at least once a week to get a shampoo and a set. She was such a sweetheart. She had Bubba Gene when she was quite a bit older. When she realized she was terminally ill, she asked me to keep an eye on him." Sunny gave Landry a look he couldn't quite decipher. "He's functional to the extent he can work and live by himself but he can't handle money. So she put my name on his checking account. I guess in essence that means I'm his guardian."

Maybe that wasn't binding in the legal sense of the word, but it certainly placed a huge responsibility on Sunny's shoulders.

"Let's talk this out. First they'll appoint an attorney, and then there will be a bail bond hearing. The judge will either set bail or refuse it. The next step will be an arraignment. Let me assure you that even a guy at the bottom of his law class can handle a bail hearing and an arraignment. He'll tell Bubba Gene to plead not guilty." Landry paused before continuing. "I feel sure that since a death is involved the case will be tried in Superior Court. That means we'll have time to come up with an acceptable attorney. Don't worry. It'll work out, I promise. You can take that to the bank."

Who was this man? He looked like Landry, he sounded like her favorite shampoo guy, but he was spouting terms like arraignment and Superior Court. The next thing she knew he'd be waxing rhapsodically about writs of habeas corpus.

Even in the upside-down world of Landry's transformation, one word made a huge impression on Sunny—bail.

"What will I have to do to make bail?

"More than likely it'll be cash or a bail bond. Do you have a couple hundred thousand lying around?" he asked. "In a murder case, that's probably what it will be. With a bail bond, you have to come up with ten percent and the bail bondsman puts up the rest. No matter what happens, with a bail bond you don't get the ten percent back."

"I've read the Janet Evanovich books and I've watched Dog on TV so I have a vague idea about bounty hunters, but I didn't know any of that stuff." She thought for a moment. "Do we even have bail bondsman in this county?"

"I'm sure there's one. People get bonded out all

the time. You just haven't noticed the office. Tomorrow morning before Bubba Gene's hearing we'll find it."

As much as she wanted to be independent and strong, just his use of the word "we" gave her a good feeling. Deep down she knew she could count on him.

Sunny kept telling herself that's why she let him pull her into his arms. He was dependable and responsible, and best of all, he made her safe and secure.

That wasn't the only thing that made him so attractive. He was much more than warm and fuzzy. Just looking at him elevated her temperature. He was sizzling hot, and off the charts with regard to sex appeal. He made her feel things that would make the ladies of the Methodist circle blush.

"Kiss me, right this minute," she demanded, slipping her hand to his nape.

"Yes, ma'am." He gave her a grin that was better than any aphrodisiac. "I can certainly do that." And he did, right there on the porch swing in front of God and all her neighbors.

In the logical recesses of her mind Sunny realized their relationship was moving too fast. On the minus side—they'd only had one date, he was her employee and she didn't know a darned thing about him.

However, and this was a gigantic however, Sunny suspected she'd met her soul mate. Wouldn't that be a miracle? To heck with convention and nosy neighbors and trying to control the uncontrollable. She could worry about that later.

With that thought in mind, Sunny enjoyed the erotic play of his lips, and tongue and very talented fingers.

Chapter 15

The transition from the wonder of the night before to the reality of the criminal justice system was disquieting even though Landry was a veteran of that world. He could image how it seemed to Sunny.

True to what he'd predicted, a high bail was set. The fact that the sheriff's entire family and most of the patrons of Double Date—along with their furry friends—had attended the arraignment obviously wasn't lost on the judge. And although it wasn't as much as Landry had thought, a hundred thousand dollars wasn't chicken feed.

He followed Sunny and her family and friends out of the courthouse. The sheriff was a smart man—and very aware of protocol—so he had to stay impartial. That didn't stop his wife from being front and center in the "Free Bubba Gene" movement.

For a few moments, Landry didn't know where the entourage was heading, and then it hit him—Miss Melanie's Tea Room. The image of tiny bone china cups, miniscule scones and cucumber sandwiches with the crust cut off danced through his head. He'd skipped breakfast and he was ready for something that would stick to his ribs, but he resigned himself to minus zero calories and strolled in behind the ladies.

"So," Miss Eugenie started the conversation. "Where are we going to come up with ten thousand dollars?"

"I can toss in a thousand," Miss Anna Belle said.

"Me, too." That offer came from Lily and seconded by Liza.

"I can't go that high, but I can manage five hundred," Raylene contributed.

"Pencil me in for that much," Toolie said.

In amounts varying from ten dollars to two hundred, the women at the table offered cash.

"I have about three thousand in my savings," Sunny commented. "That still leaves us short."

"Don't worry about it. I'll make up the difference." That assurance came from Anna Belle's husband, Joe Nunn. He was the spitting image of the Kentucky Colonel and one of the nicest guys Landry had ever met.

"Our problem now is to get him a decent lawyer," Joe continued. The women nodded in agreement.

They didn't realize Landry had an ace up his sleeve—his law partner and best friend, Colby Wharton—who, incidentally, had a license to practice law in Texas.

That would remain his secret, at least for a little while, Landry thought as he slipped away in search of a phone. It was time to call off the bet and bring in the cavalry.

Landry's biggest problem was how to pull this off without sending Sunny into orbit.

"Hey, Colby. How are things going?"

"Pretty good, what's up?"

"Call me back. We need to have a talk." Landry gave him the number of the telephone at the library. After a lengthy search he'd discovered it was the only working pay phone in town. The one at the convenience

Ann DeFee

store was missing the receiver. What he wouldn't give for the cell phone he'd left in New Orleans.

"Okay," Colby agreed without hesitation.

Landry knew his friend wouldn't let him down.

After Landry explained the problem and outlined his plan, Colby agreed to return to Texas to try the case.

"You're damned lucky I'm finishing up my current case. You've been down there less than three weeks and you're already knee-deep in a murder. I suppose you don't want to discuss our bet, huh?" Colby laughed at his own humor.

"Not right now. When can you get down here?"

"Give me a week or two. Things move slowly in Port Serenity. I suspect we won't go to trial for a long time, and I have a couple of things to finish here. You can prepare our strategy," Colby said. "You're better at that kind of thing than I am. But, I'll send Pete and Jillian down to get the investigation started."

"Okay. Have them bring my wallet. I need my credit cards."

Colby's raucous laughter reverberated through the phone.

Landry made a rude remark that caused his partner to laugh even louder.

When Colby finally got himself under control, he delved into the details.

"Pete and Jillian will be down there day after tomorrow. They'll contact you."

"Make sure they do it on the QT."

"Sure. I can tell you're not in the mood to reveal your identity to the cute little blond, correct?"

"I'm afraid so. At least, not now."

100

"Got it," Colby said, chuckling again. "You're about to get your platinum card back."

When he started humming, "You're in the money," Landry pushed the disconnect button.

Chapter 16

It had been two days since the bail bond hearing and the arraignment—two very long days. Bubba Gene had been bonded out and was living in Miss Anna Belle's guest house. He'd also resumed his janitorial duties at the salon.

Sunny had been so busy she hadn't had much time to worry about what was happening at work, or to find out what Landry was doing. His sudden disappearance from the tearoom was strange, but even more confusing was the fact he was making himself scarce. Every time she had a minute to talk, he made an excuse to leave. How could he avoid her after what they'd experienced on her porch swing? Was it a typical male "let's not talk about it," or was it something else?

The last customer had just left and Sunny was in the process of locking up when she spotted Landry walking toward the beach. Not that she was spying on him—honestly she wasn't—but she couldn't force herself away from the window.

Landry walked—amend that to sauntered, and Lord could that man saunter—toward the gazebo where he met two people. It was obvious he knew them because he shook the man's hand and hugged the woman. Warning signs went up all over the place. Other than her friends, family and customers, Sunny didn't think he knew anyone in Port Serenity, and she didn't recognize that couple.

Should she ask Sheriff Dave to run a background check on her boyfriend, employee or whatever you wanted to call him? Oh, definitely yes. Making the assumption that Uncle Dave would handle the matter with finesse, Sunny picked up the phone. "I need a favor."

Landry felt good following his meeting with Pete and Jillian. If it was possible to get to the bottom of the situation, they were the team to do it. They were the best investigators in the firm. And to make things even better, they'd brought him his platinum American Express and his debit card.

Hip, hip hooray! Landry's days as a shampoo guy were numbered; so in the interest of preserving his fledgling relationship with Sunny, he had to do some fast courting. A romantic date was the ticket. However, he couldn't magically come up with money, at least not until he explained the situation. Damn that bet!

Once a lie got legs, it took off and was almost impossible to run down. Sunny was worth whatever he had to do, up to and including some fancy-knee walking. Landry was contemplating the problem when Raylene joined him in the break room.

"Hey, good looking. What's with the big frown?"

"I want to take Sunny on a romantic date. But with the Bubba Gene situation I'm not sure what I should do." Landry finished his thought by holding up his hands.

"Oh, sugar, I get it. She definitely needs something to get her mind off her problems." Raylene assumed the Thinker pose. "Let me ponder this situation. We need candles and wine but you're on a beer budget. Not having wheels is a bit of a problem, too."

103

Landry felt like a heel, but he let Raylene continue her brainstorming.

"A hamburger and a beer at the Dew Drop Inn won't work. So—" Raylene tapped her knuckles on the table. "I've got it."

Landry almost jumped out of his skin when his coconspirator yelled, "Toolie, come back here, girl."

Great! Just what he needed—someone else in the loop.

"Keep your shirt on, I'll be there in a second," Toolie yelled back.

Those two never used their inside voices.

"Where's the fire?" Toolie asked, smart-mouthed as usual.

"Landry needs some dating advice."

"What?"

"You heard me. The dude doesn't have any cash but he wants to make a good impression on you know who." Raylene nodded in the direction of the front counter and ended her explanation with a wink and a grin.

Toolie retrieved a Dr. Pepper from the refrigerator and popped the top. "Let me think." She rolled the can across her forehead as if she was participating in a mind-reading gig.

"How about this? The Kiwanis Fish Fry," she suggested.

"You have *got* to kidding me." Landry couldn't suppress a snort. "Isn't that a bit...fishy."

The women ignored his pun.

"I love them hush puppies," Bubba Gene said.

He'd joined them and was leaning on his broom, a big smile on his face. "Aunt Hallie used to make hush puppies, ya know that?"

Sooner, rather than later, Landry had to have a long talk with Bubba Gene. Somewhere in his memory the man had the key to crime; Landry just had to ferret it out.

However, his concern of the moment was how to romance the boss. So it was back to discussing the Kiwanis Fish Fry.

"It'll work. I know it will," Raylene exclaimed.

Uh-oh. She was getting enthusiastic, and that might not be a good thing.

"It only costs $5.95 a person and it's all you can eat catfish and hush puppies. It's held at the beach with lanterns and everything. You can even rent a kayak. What could be more romantic than a moonlight float on the bay?"

The catfish cuisine part was dicey. A relaxing kayak trip had possibilities.

When Landry suggested the fish fry, Sunny jumped at the chance to be with him again. It was a real date, with a meal he was going to pay for—even if it did cost a whoppin' big $5.95. So what if her uncle was doing a background check on him? But with everything she had on her plate, including being worried sick about Bubba Gene, she didn't have time for dating.

Who *was* she kidding?

Sunny's bedroom looked like a bargain basement dressing room after a clearance sale. Practically every piece of clothing she owned was on the floor or on the bed. She picked up a cotton sundress and tossed it toward the closet.

Jeans? Maybe. Halter top? T-shirt? No. She dug through her closet until she discovered a daisy yellow skirt, a matching camisole and her new wedgie sandals. Bingo!

Sunny had just added a final spray of perfume when the doorbell rang. Wow—good looking, sexy and punctual. What a combo!

And "wow" didn't come close to describing the guy standing at her door. What had happened to the ever-present jeans and T-shirt?

"You look great." In fact, he was a sight to behold in a pair of Dockers and a pale blue polo.

"Thanks, and may I say that you're gorgeous."

Sunny couldn't put her finger on what was happening between them. For some reason they were behaving as if this was a blind date, and that was so far from the truth it wasn't even funny.

She knew why she was acting weird. It was his clandestine meeting in the park. There had to be an innocent reason. Right? And there was a wetland in the Mojave for sale. Of course that was her funky inner voice talking, and she always tried to ignore that pest.

"Hey, big guy, I need a kiss," she demanded, grabbing the placket of his shirt and pulling him inside.

"I'm always ready to serve," he said, flashing a grin that could curl her toes. Then he laid a kiss on her that truly did curl her toes.

"I think we should get going while we still can."

"Uh-huh." She somehow managed to express

agreement without licking her lips. Would wonders never cease?

The Kiwanis Fish Fry was the service club's annual fund-raiser. It was also one of the biggest social events of the summer. Volunteers were manning deep-fat fryers containing enough catfish and hush puppies to feed a horde. Other members were dishing up side dishes and hosting the beer garden.

"This is fun," Landry admitted after he'd polished off a heaping plate of food.

"I like it." She paused and then asked the question she'd been pondering. "Exactly where are you from?"

He waited a moment before answering. "New Orleans. That's where I was born." He didn't elaborate as he tossed their dinner debris in the trash and led her down the beach toward the swampy area of the bay.

"Where are we going?" Sunny's curiosity was about to get the best of her.

"We're going for a romantic kayak ride. I need some privacy to tell you something."

"How about a kiss?"

"That might be a little more difficult in a kayak."

Landry helped Sunny into the boat and then squeezed in with her.

"I hope you know what you're doing." She hadn't been in a kayak in ages, so she was counting on his expertise.

"I think I do."

"Ooh-kay, that gives me a great deal of confidence," Sunny really wasn't as bothered as she sounded. She could swim, the water was fairly tranquil and there were a ton of people on the shore.

Landry paddled toward the swamp, allowing the kayak to drift under a canopy of low-hanging trees.

"We need to talk."

Under the best of circumstances, those were not words that evoked a great sense of optimism. Oh, well. If it was going to be awful, Sunny figured she could at least enjoy the moonlight.

Sunny, I'm not—"

She failed to hear the rest of the sentence because his words were obliterated in a haze of pure terror. There was a snake hanging in the tree, right above her head.

A snake! A SNAKE!

Sheer horror blossomed into full-blown hysteria when she heard a loud plop and went eyeball to eyeball with a serpent.

Folks in Houston probably heard her screech.

Before Landry could figure out what was happening, Sunny had flipped the kayak and they were both treading water.

"Hang on," he ordered. "Can you swim?"

Instead of answering, she was off like a shot toward the beach.

She wasn't exactly the most graceful swimmer he'd ever seen, but she was pretty darned fast.

Landry had been on a swim team in high school so he was able to catch up with her. Her eyes were the size of dinner plates, her arms were flailing, and the only word she uttered was *snake* before she shot off like an Olympic contender.

Now he understood. It was time to put on the gas. Reptiles, particularly those of the aquatic variety, were not among his favorite critters.

Talk about an understatement!

In their frantic race back to civilization, Landry and Sunny made quite a bit of noise. By the time they stepped onto dry land they had garnered an audience. A kind soul provided a couple of blankets that smelled suspiciously like a wet dog.

Sunny had regained her sense of humor by the time they returned to her home. "Miss Priss won't have anything to do with me." Her calico cat took one sniff, disdainfully pointed her nose in the air, and disappeared off the porch.

Sunny leaned over to smell Landry's shirt. "Ooh, yeech. We'll put our clothes in the washer and then take a shower. How does that grab you?" she asked with an eyebrow wiggle.

Apparently it grabbed him just fine—thank you very much—because he pulled her into his arms, nibbled all the way up her neck, and then proceeded to feast on her lips.

When they finally came up for a breath, Sunny's sense of propriety kicked in. She realized they had two options. Number one, stop what they were doing, or number two, go inside. Being the sensible, strong, independent woman that she was, she chose the second. Oh, yeah!

"Inside," Sunny demanded, pointing toward the front door.

"Your wish is…"

Sunny didn't even allow him to finish his sentence. Without her knowledge or consent, her new motto had become more action, fewer words. She grabbed a handful of his blue polo and pulled him into her house, ready and more than willing to have her way with him. Not that he seemed the least bit averse to the whole idea.

The minute they cleared the portal, he backed her up against the door and slid the bolt to the locked position. And that was the start of Sunny's initiation into the true world of making love. Her entire relationship with Walter had been a sham on every level, particularly intimacy.

She knew she was a goner when Landry nestled his leg between her thighs. He made quick work of the buttons down the front of her skirt. It fell into a puddle by her feet, leaving only a thin scrap of material between the most sensitive of places and the rough denim of his leg. All cogent thought went bye-bye when he pulled her stretchy camisole up and over her little lacy Victoria's Secret bra and proceeded to lick, suckle and generally drive her wild.

Never in Sunny's wildest dreams had she ever considered making love on the Aubusson carpet in her foyer.

But that's exactly what she did, and savored every minute of it!

Chapter 17

Landry was still sporting a goofy grin when he woke up in Sunny's bedroom at the crack of dawn. The place was so girly it made his testosterone sit up and take notice.

He took a quick survey of his surroundings—the four poster bed, acres of fluffy white material, and enough pillows to stock a mattress store. As far as decorating went, it was worthy of a Southern Living photo shoot.

His bed partner was stunning. Not only was she gorgeous, she looked well-loved. A grin played across Landry's face. He was responsible for all that mussed hair and her slightly puffy lips. Guilty as charged and proud of it!

"Hey, peaches," he whispered as he nuzzled her neck. Peaches fit her to a T. She had a peaches-and-cream complexion, and soft blond hair, and man, oh man, was she ever luscious.

"Hmm," she mumbled. He took that as his invitation to kiss her into the new morning.

Much, much later Landry was still thinking about his incredible luck as he drifted back to sleep.

Sunny was in the middle of a scrumptious dream when an annoying bell kept intruding. In the fuzzy depths of sleep, she thought it was her alarm clock, and for some reason she couldn't turn it off. But when reality intruded, she realized it was the telephone.

What kind of apocalyptic news was ready to

pounce? It was too early in the morning for ugly thoughts so she swatted them away.

When she rolled over, Sunny was more than a little aware of the man in her bed. He was adorable—almost boyish in his deep sleep. She could attest to the fact he was anything but boyish.

Resisting the urge to run her fingers through the crinkly hair on his chest, she grabbed the cordless phone.

It was Uncle Dave. "Hey, sweetheart, I have some news about Landry."

That woke her up. "What?" She grabbed her robe and was halfway down the stairs before Dave could continue.

"He's a criminal defense attorney in New Orleans."

"He's a what?" she squeaked. Under normal circumstances, she was the pragmatic, careful one. So how had he managed to get under her defenses? And what was he doing in Port Serenity?

"Do you remember Colby Wharton?"

Of course she did. She went to high school with him and his folks owned half the town. "What's he got to do with this?"

"He's Landry's law partner."

"I'm gonna kill him."

"Kill Colby?"

"Of course not, but Landry Valliere is a dead man."

"You want me to do it for you?"

The offer was certainly tempting, not that he was serious. "You're my favorite uncle; you know that, don't you?"

"Don't let your uncle Joe hear that," he said with a laugh.

"Yeah, but I still love you."

"Are you okay?"

"Absolutely. Tell Aunt Eugenie I'll call her later."

"Will do. Don't do anything I wouldn't do."

Sunny hit the disconnect button and stalked back up the stairs. She was ready, willing and able to do some whoop-ass on the dude in her bed.

Landry was still asleep. That was good, especially since he was at least a foot taller and eighty pounds heavier than she was. She doubted very seriously he'd take a pummeling lying down—no pun intended.

Sunny had to admit she was glad he was on the right side of the law. But he'd led her to believe he was down on his luck. Homeless, her rear end. The guy was probably rich—weren't those attorney types all rolling in dough? And could she possibly be any more of a naïve country girl?

Fueled by her ire, Sunny pounced on her victim, landing in the middle of his delicious chest. She was, oh so, tempted to pop him in the nose. No, no, no. First and foremost she was a lady—somehow she had to dredge up a modicum of restraint.

"You're a scum-sucking liar," Sunny punctuated her declaration by tweaking his chest hair.

"Damn, that hurts!" He went from a deep sleep to being wide awake in two-point-two seconds.

"You said you needed a job, and to that I say kiss

my white rear-end."

"Okay, I get it." He sat up, tossing her from her perch and scooting toward the headboard.

"You've obviously talked to someone," he said with a sigh.

"Yes, sir. I did."

He reached out to stroke her cheek, but retracted his hand when she hit him.

"Here's the truth and nothing but the truth. I promise." He crossed an X on his chest. "It started on a dark and lonely night."

Sunny responded with a nasty look.

"Honestly, it did. Here goes." Then he confessed everything from the inception of the wager to the present.

In a way, she was relieved. At least his picture wasn't on a post office wall. But, he had a bet with his law partner! Talk about chutzpah. And what was going to happen to them? That is if there was a "them".

Landry was a city boy. He couldn't possibly be happy in Port Serenity, not for any extended period of time. Instinctively Sunny had known from the beginning that he'd turn her life upside down. She'd been right about that.

Would he stay or would he go? Was he rich or was he struggling financially? She didn't have an answer to any of those questions. Things were so topsy-turvy, she couldn't tell up from down.

The only silver lining was that he'd promised to help Bubba Gene. And there was the fact she'd just had the most incredible night of her life.

Don't go there! She had to concentrate on Bubba

Gene. Considering the circumstantial evidence against him, he was going to need all the help he could get. And that's where Landry came in.

A little bit of God's meddling would be appreciated, too.

Landry felt better than he had in weeks. There was something to be said for confession. Now, if he could decipher what Sunny was thinking. Her face was normally an open book. Too bad she'd decided to go for stoic this time.

None of that mattered because he was determined to turn their relationship into something lasting. Looking at the situation realistically, he knew he had a huge job ahead of him. That didn't matter because when Mr. Most Eligible Bachelor fell, he toppled like a ton of bricks.

"I know you have a lot to think about, so for now, I'll leave you alone." He stood, pulling her to her feet. "I have to go back to my office in New Orleans for a couple of days, but I'm not giving up on us. I promise." He emphasized the vow with a long, hot, mind-blowing kiss, and leaned his forehead against hers.

"Sweetheart," he continued, "I'd better leave while I still can." He gently swatted her on the butt. "But I can't go without my pants."

"Oops. They're in the dryer."

Chapter 18

Sunny's emotions were ping-ponging as she watched Landry stroll down the sidewalk. She believed him when he said he wasn't walking out on her. On the contrary, as obstinate as he was, he was probably making plans to camp out in the middle of her life.

What to do, what to do? Sunny grabbed the phone and called in the troops.

"Hey, Liza, can you meet me for lunch? And bring Lily with you."

"Need I ask if we're having a crisis?" her cousin asked with a giggle.

Oh, boy, news of their impromptu water dunking had probably spread like wildfire. "How about meeting me at the Beachfront Inn around one o'clock?"

"Yes, ma'am," Liza said, ruining her serious answer by breaking into laughter.

Sunny's next call was to Raylene to let her know she'd be late and Landry wouldn't be in at all. She made assurances she'd be in time to help with Traci Manning—aka Bridezilla—and her six attendants, scheduled for ten o'clock.

Just the thought of that appointment gave her a headache. "Do you have the champagne chilled?"

"Ab-so-lutely. Survival is the name of *this* game," Raylene responded.

Just as Sunny suspected, Traci alternately cried, giggled and issued orders. That was after consuming half a magnum of champagne. Short of stealing the bottle, Sunny couldn't keep the bubbly out of the girl's hands. From the looks of things, all the ladies had been

tippling well before they'd showed up at Double Date.
     Ye Gods!

     Before the styling debacle was finished, the
mother-in-law was blotto, the bridesmaids were about to
mutiny, the bride had spent a good deal of time in the
restroom purging her meal, and Sunny had a raging
headache. However, that wasn't the worst of it.
     Sunny's biggest problem was that the bride
walked out of the salon with hair the color of an
overcooked beet. She was a walking advertisement for
salon malpractice. And it wasn't their fault, no way! Still
if they didn't get hauled into court, it would be a
miracle.
     "Remind me never to serve adult beverages to a
bridal party, ever again."
     "Right on, boss. Keep in mind that you told her
over and over what would happen if you put red/violet
dye on her blond hair."
     "I know. But I could have refused to do the color
and I should have told her to go somewhere else,"
Sunny wailed, wringing her hands.
     "She outweighed you by a good fifty pounds. I
remember her from junior high," Raylene ruminated.
"Even then she was as mean as a junkyard dog. That girl
didn't hesitant to take on anyone who didn't toe her line.
Personally, I don't think you had a choice."
     Sunny slumped in her chair. "Intellectually I
know all that. I just…" She shook her head in disgust.
"What are people gonna think?"
     "They're going to think she's a fruitcake,"
Toolie offered. "When those two bridesmaids started

117

yelling at each other about high school boyfriends, I was laughing so hard I thought I'd pee my pants."

Sunny couldn't resist a giggle. "I'm going to meet my cousins for lunch." She grabbed her purse. "I've got to get out of here. Are you sure you don't need me for a couple of hours?"

"Nope, you go have some girl talk. We heard about your dip in the bay." In unison Raylene and Toolie broke into belly laughs.

"If a really big snake fell on your kayak you'd be in the water before you could spit." Sunny barely resisted the urge to stick out her tongue.

"Probably," Toolie agreed. "I don't even like worms."

"So get going. We're fine." Raylene shooed her boss out the door.

The Beachfront Inn was de rigueur with the Junior League crowd. It was the only place in town that served icy mimosas, wine spritzers, Earl Grey tea and tiny sandwiches. How girly-girl was that?

Under normal circumstances, Sunny didn't patronize the Inn. Their meals were barely big enough to keep a caterpillar alive. But these weren't normal times, and frankly, she wasn't up for the clatter and noise of the café.

"Hey, sweetie." Liz gave her a hug before she sat down. "Lily will be here in a few minutes. We're dying to hear what happened last night. Charlie was at the fish fry, and he said you kept muttering something about a snake. I hope you weren't talking about your date. I think he's cute."

So did Sunny, and that wasn't the problem. She was trying to come up with an intelligent comment when Lily arrived and the hugging ritual started all over.

Sunny had never been able to put anything over on her cousins, so she spilled her guts—everything from his profession, to the bet, to the...well, she didn't quite tell them everything. But she did say enough that they got the picture.

"Oh. My. God! I think I'm having a hot flash," Liza exclaimed before she chugged half a glass of sweet tea. "It's been forever since..."

"I know, honey." Lily patted her sister's hand. After Liza's husband died she'd refused to get back in the dating scene.

"Now we can live vicariously through our favorite brat," Lily said.

"I'm not a brat," Sunny's protestation was like fluff in the wind. "And you're happily married."

She didn't ask her cousins for advice about Landry; she didn't have to. Just talking it out had cleared her mind. It assured her that if she didn't let their relationship—or whatever it was—run its course, she'd regret it forever. So she had to give fate a green light.

"I hate to bring up an unpleasant subject while we're enjoying a mimosa, but what do you guys really think happened to Aunt Hallie?" Lily asked. "And an even bigger question is what else can we do to help Bubba Gene? Bailing him out was just the first step. We still have to find a good attorney. *And* I think we need to do some sleuthing of our own."

"Landry didn't specifically say so, but I'm pretty sure his partner, Colby Wharton, is planning to act as

Bubba Gene's attorney. That's one huge worry down. So what kind of sleuthing are we talking about?" Sunny asked. Although she was loath to admit it, she'd always harbored a desire to be a detective.

Apparently Liza had read a couple of Nancy Drew novels herself. "Rumor has it that one of those big-box shopping centers is being proposed for the land between Aunt Hallie's place and old man Haradway's swamp."

"Wasn't it Crumpy Hardaway's idiot grandson who tried to rob you?" Lily asked. Before Sunny could respond, her cousin continued. "And what was with the tea towel? Lord in heaven, couldn't the boy buy a ski mask?"

"Uncle Dave said he was going for the Ku Klux Klan look," Sunny said, shaking her head. "He couldn't be the murderer. He's in jail, although he does have several brothers, so I guess it's possible one of them had something to do with Aunt Hallie's death."

The cousins were contemplating the lack of Hardaway gray matter when Liza spoke up. "Okay, back to the land deal, Charlie's roommate from Texas A&M is a partner in one of the giant development companies in Houston. They're the folks who want to build the shopping center. He said that Walter is up to his kneecaps in the arrangement."

"Walter? My Walter?"

"Walter Harrington," Liza said in her best lawyer voice. "Do you want Charlie to get more information?"

Not only were Liza and Lily on opposite ends of the spectrum looks-wise, their selection of profession couldn't have been any more different. Liza was a land-

use attorney, who along with her pal Charlie Taylor had
established a real estate development company. Lily, on
the other hand, owned a boutique on Main Street
appropriately named Miss Scarlett's Boudoir.

Sunny's mind was spinning a mile a minute. "I
don't want to make life difficult for Walter. I'm positive
he didn't have anything to do with Aunt Hallie's death.
When we were married I couldn't even get him to kill a
spider." She shook her head. "Nope, he's not involved.
So let's think about the Hardaway's. Do you think one
of them could have killed Aunt Hallie to keep her from
selling? Or conversely, they wanted her to sell, and she
wouldn't."

"Who knows? They're certainly not very bright,"
Liza answered.

Sunny rubbed the bridge of her nose where a
headache had taken up residence. "It sounds possible,
but, I don't know. It doesn't feel right. There was
something really personal about the way she was killed."

On the one hand, the Hardaway's probably
wouldn't want a shopping center cozied up next to the
family home. But if you looked at it in terms of money,
they'd be rich enough they wouldn't have to rob
convenience stores—or beauty salons.

"How about this for an idea?"

Sunny's ears perked up. Leave it to Liza to come
up with a solution. She'd always been the family
problem solver.

"Between the three of us, we know every gossip
in town. We'll have some well-placed conversations
and, you know—" she shrugged and grinned "—sort of

121

lay out our suspicions. Then we sit back and see what pops up."

The woman was a genius. Although Landry's professional investigators were undoubtedly excellent, they weren't good old boys, or girls, and the natives would never spill their guts to them.

"I think that's a great idea," Sunny said.

Lily lifted her hand for a high-five. "Me, too."

"Now, let's talk logistics," Liza always went straight for the nitty-gritty. "We should consider the possibility we're about to tweak the tail of a tiger."

"Oh, fiddle dee dee." Spoken as only the owner of Scarlett's Boudoir could. "No one in Port Serenity would dare lay a pinkie on us. Not with Uncle Dave in our corner."

"That's probably what Aunt Hallie thought," Liza reminded them.

Sunny was so busy thinking about her ex that she didn't comment. Could Walter be desperate enough to get away from his mother that he'd do something illegal? Naw—Walter didn't have the guts.

Chapter 20

Two days had passed since Sunny's lunch with Lily and Liza. Not surprisingly, they'd been able to implement their plan with ease. It helped that they had complete access to the town's leading salon and to the store that every woman in the county patronized. Sunny planted the seed with a couple of unrepentant gossips, and no telling how many people Lily had cornered.

It had been forty-eight hours since Sunny had heard from Landry. Darn it—she knew he was in New Orleans on business, but she missed him something fierce. Good employees were hard to come by and acceptable boyfriends were even more difficult to find.

Fortunately, she was saved by the bell; that would be the front-door chime announcing the arrival of the dingbat duo—Raylene and Toolie.

"Hey, boss lady, what's on the schedule for today?" Toolie asked, turning the appointment book around so she could read it.

"Please tell me I don't have to cut Mrs. Stackhouse's hair." Toolie hit her forehead with her palm. "It's simply not fair."

Sunny couldn't resist a grin. "The customer is always right at Double Date."

Raylene gave an irreverent snort. "Some of our patrons are two enchiladas short of a combo plate."

"I'll give you that one," Sunny conceded, adding a giggle.

Velda Stackhouse was truly one of a kind. Invariably she came into the salon with dots painted all over her face—one dot on her forehead for the length of her bangs and matching dots on her chin and neck for the location of her layers. When all was said and done the dots were supposed to connect. And lately she'd been putting polka dots on her poodle prior to his grooming.

Fruitcake city!

That bit of levity gave Sunny a much-needed reprieve from thinking about Landry. As much as she trusted Raylene and Toolie, she hadn't confided her concerns about him or the murder. What could she say? *I'm pretty sure I'm falling in love with our shampoo guy, who by the way is a criminal defense attorney. And my cousins and I are trying to flush out a killer*. Even for Raylene and Toolie, that was too much information.

"Where's Landry this morning?" Raylene asked.

"He's uh…" Sunny's explanation was cut short when the subject of their conversation strolled in the back door. There he was, just as pretty as you please— faded jeans, scuffed boots, sexy grin and gorgeous green eyes.

"Ladies, are we having a staff meeting?" It was an ordinary question, but his velvety baritone made her think of hot fudge melting on homemade ice cream.

Yummy and decadent.

"Not without you, big guy," Toolie answered. "I was just griping about one of my clients."

Sunny was surprised that Toolie hadn't reverted to the junior high flirtation of a combination hair flip and giggle. As it was, she managed only the giggle.

"Landry, may I speak to you for a moment?" Sunny asked. Raylene and Toolie hadn't moved an inch. "Privately."

"Sure." He gave her another one of *those* grins. "Ladies, I'll be back in a few minutes."

Her employees finally took the hint and wandered toward their stations.

To Landry's credit, he waited until they were out of sight before he nibbled on Sunny's ear.

"What can I do for you?" he asked.

"Stop that," Sunny halfheartedly admonished him. "What are you doing here?"

"This is my place of employment, don't you remember?"

Sunny took his hand and pulled him out the front door. "Let's go to the park. We need to talk."

"Okey, dokey," he agreed. "After you."

Sunny was in the mood for stomping; however, Landry was more into strolling. So they strolled all the way to the gazebo. He sat down on the bench and stretched out his long legs.

The man was very comfortable in his own skin.

"I wasn't positive you'd come back to work. Not with the bet, and Aunt Hallie's murder, and everything." Sunny waved her hands to encompass the problems of the world, or at least her part of the planet.

"Sweetheart, I told you I wasn't going away. I simply had to go to New Orleans to discuss the case with Colby." He picked up her hand and kissed the base of each finger.

Wowzer! He could do that again, and again, and again.

"You remember Colby, don't you?"

"Sure." How could she forget Colby Wharton? The guy had been the super stud of Port Serenity High

School when Sunny was a lowly freshman. That hadn't made them social equals—not by a long shot.

"Actually, I don't know him, but I know of him." She laughed, thinking about all the girls who'd had crushes on him. "He was a major heartthrob."

"Really?" Landry's grin spread over his entire face. "I'll have to rib him about that."

"Is he married?"

"Don't go there, little missy," he emphasized his command with one of those kisses that made Sunny think of romantic nights. Were public displays of affection legal in Port Serenity? Who knew, and even more importantly, who cared?

"Just for your edification, he's not married. The important thing is he's a member of the Texas Bar. So he can try Bubba Gene's case."

"That's great, I guess." Sunny had to wonder how successful their law firm was if they were able to drop everything and come to Port Serenity.

"It's better than great, because other than me he's the best."

Just the fact that someone competent was willing to help Bubba Gene gave Sunny a boost.

"Speaking of your employment, should I put up my Help Wanted sign?"

Landry gave her a grin. "Hang loose for a week or two. I'm having fun with you guys. This is a long-delayed vacation."

Sunny gave him a friendly punch on the arm. "You have a weird sense of fun. Most people go to Maui for a vacation."

"But I wouldn't have met you if I'd gone to Hawaii."

Yep, that was the truth and nothing but the truth.

The remainder of the day was uneventful; that is, until the mail came and things went south.

If there was such a thing as a classic threatening note, the one Sunny received would qualify. It showed up in an innocuous white envelope and was mailed from the main post office. The text was cut out of the newspaper, and the sentiment was more than a bit chilling.

"This, this…piece of garbage says *Stop meddling, bitch*," Sunny exclaimed, barely suppressing an unladylike expletive. She hadn't been the recipient of a threatening note since the eighth grade, and that one had been from her rival for cheerleader.

"Put it on the counter, and don't touch it. Raylene, call the Sheriff," Landry instructed. "This isn't a joke."

Toolie was about to hyperventilate, and Raylene wasn't faring much better; however, she managed to grab the phone and make the call.

When Sunny took a deep breath and regained control of her emotions, she realized one thing. Their well-placed questions had prompted someone to take action.

Landry was *not* going to be happy when he discovered what they'd been up to. But on the bright side; if they found the note writer, they would unmask the killer.

And for sure it wasn't Bubba Gene. He couldn't

Ann DeFee

spell *bitch* if his life depended on it.

Chapter 21

News of Sunny's note went through the family like a wildfire in West Texas. True to form, Lily was the first to call.

"I want you and Landry to come for supper." The invitation felt more like a command than a friendly request. At first glance Lily might appear to be a ditzy blond. However, the term *steel magnolia* was custom made for her.

"Liza will be here. We're due for a war council." Lily had obviously jumped to the same conclusion Sunny had. Someone in town was getting nervous. So what should they do about it? Pull the tiger's tail again?

"Do we really have to get the guys involved?"

"Yes." Lily didn't elaborate before she hung up. That girl was a natural-born steamroller.

There's something I need to tell you before we get to Lily's house." They were in Landry's rental car, and Sunny had finally decided she had to tell him the whole story.

"Sounds like this might give me heartburn." Landry's bone-melting smile tempered his comment.

"Well," Sunny started to sugar coat her confession, but at the last minute went for full disclosure.

He slammed on the brakes and pulled to the curb. "You guys did what?"

"We asked some leading questions. I think they got to the right person, prompting him or her to send that threatening note."

"Good God!"

"What can I say?" Sunny said somewhat sheepishly. "All's not quiet on the home front."

"This is not funny, Sunny," Landry retorted, giving her a glare. After a few seconds, he put the car in gear and pulled into the traffic.

He was not happy, and she couldn't blame him. Interfering in a murder investigation wasn't the smartest stunt they'd ever pulled.

Dinner was a cordial affair; primarily due to the fact the conversation revolved around casual topics. It was Clay who finally got down to business.

"I talked to Dave. He's beyond pissed at you girls."

"Call me surprised," Sunny said. "Uncle Dave takes his oath to protect and serve seriously, especially when it comes to his family.

"So, you talked to *my uncle*?" Lily speared her husband with a look that could be accomplished only in a long-term marriage.

"Sure did."

"And you didn't discuss it with me first."

"Nope."

Brave man.

"Never mind that," Liza said. "We have to come up with a game plan, and Sunny's safety is primary. Does anyone have an idea?"

Landry had a strategy in mind, but he wasn't sure Sunny would want it aired in front of her family.

He wondered how she'd feel about a live-in bodyguard—him, of course. That discussion, however, required more privacy than they had at the moment.

His hand was on her thigh so he gave her a little squeeze. Initially it was an effort to comfort her. Then it quickly changed into something more sensual. It didn't take much for his heart to start racing and other body parts to come to full attention.

"Landry and I have to talk." Sunny jumped up, pulling him with her. "We're going to the porch," she said to her hostess. "I'll be back to help you with the dishes."

She was halfway out the door before Landry could catch up. He didn't think they could do what he *really* wanted to do on the front porch swing. *That* would land him in the county jail.

Sunny couldn't believe what she was about to suggest. Sure, she was nervous about the note. However, she recognized an opportunity when it dropped in her lap.

"I'd like for you to move into my house."

Landry sat down on the porch swing with a thud. She'd beat him to the punch.

"Really?"

Sunny joined him on the swing. "You can sleep on the couch is you want."

"You've got to be kidding."

"Well. . ."

Sunny didn't get the chance to answer before he covered her mouth with his, giving her a long, lazy summertime kiss that went on forever.

Sorry to say, that was as hot as it was going to get on Lily's front porch.

"Is that a yes?" she asked, when they finally took a break.

"Absolutely. And no couch."

"No couch."

"What are you planning to tell your cousins?"

"How about the truth?"

"Sounds like a plan to me," he agreed, following her back into the house. He certainly hoped Clay didn't pull out his twelve-gauge shotgun. That would be a real downer.

"Here's the deal," Sunny said.

Lily interrupted her cousin's explanation by handing her a plate heaped with dessert.

Hmmm, chocolate cream pie, her favorite. Explanations could wait, Sunny thought, her mouth watering at the mere idea of sticking a fork into all that yummy whipped cream.

Landry obviously wasn't distracted by the chocolate pie. "I'm planning to move in with Sunny until we figure out what's going on," he announced."

At his statement, several forks stopped in midair. Clay, however, was the first to speak.

"Is that right?"

"Yes, and I don't want to hear any garbage about it," Sunny said around a mouthful of pie.

Clay waved his hands in surrender. "You won't hear a word from me. I can't guarantee what Anna Belle, Joe, Eugenie or Sheriff Dave's gonna say."

Sunny shot Landry an apologetic look. "I'll talk

to them," she said, glancing at each of her relatives. "Your job is to make sure that news of my new roomie doesn't hit the grapevine."

"We can try," Liza agreed. "But you have the nosiest neighbors in town, so I wouldn't plan on keeping anything secret. Perhaps, that's not all bad. If our perp realizes you're living with someone he'll leave you alone."

"So now that your bodyguard is in place, what are we going to do about the threats?" Lily asked.

"I think we should let Uncle Dave do his job," Sunny said. "The murderer is obviously someone we know. That's unfortunate because everyone in town was praying it would be a transient. I think it's important we keep this note a secret. That'll give the police a chance to do their job without interference. Perhaps they can get some fingerprints, or something, off it."

"Right on," Liza said and everyone nodded in agreement.

"That wasn't too bad, at least not for an inquisition," Landry commented as they drove toward his apartment above Double Date to pack his belongings.

"I'm sorry you had to suffer through my relatives' questions.

"No problem, none at all." He shot her a sexy wink. "Especially since I get to move in with you."

"Yeah." Sunny hated to admit she was having doubts about the wisdom of her idea. What *would* people think? Absolutely nothing got by her neighbors; and news of a guy moving into Chez McAllister would

Ann DeFee

spread like wildfire. Should she worry about it now, or
should she think about it later?

Later—definitely.

Chapter 22

Sunny felt like a voyeur as she helped him pack his clothes. He looked darned good in a pair of jeans; and he'd been even more handsome in the borrowed duds he wore to the wedding. She couldn't wait to see him in the expensive wool suit she was fondling. It felt like cashmere and it certainly wasn't an off-the-rack garment. So what was his financial situation? Not that it was any of her business. Yeah, right.

"Do you have everything?"

"Yep," he said, stowing the suits in a garment bag. "Now I do. Are you ready?"

That was an interesting question.

"Uh-huh." Sunny barely resisted the urge to bat her eyelashes. Coquettishness had never been her style. She was more of a "full guns blazing" kind of girl. "Let's go home."

"I'm positive I left my front porch light on. I always do," Sunny said as they pulled into the driveway of her bungalow.

"It's probably burned out."

"I suppose I'm being skittish. Why don't you park here?" She indicated a spot near the front sidewalk. "After we unload, you can move your car to the garage.

Sunny had purchased her home shortly after the salon started showing a profit, and she loved it. Built in the early part of the twentieth century it had white clapboard siding, glossy black shutters, a wraparound porch and a cozy setting of white wicker furniture. Harper Lee would have felt right at home.

Although the gas lamp in the yard did little to illuminate the front door, something didn't feel right to Sunny.

Landry turned off the engine and gave her an appraising look. "You're not comfortable with this, are you?"

Sunny realized he thought she was having second thoughts about his moving in. In response, she put her hand on his arm.

"It's not you, definitely not you. I just think there's something amiss, and I'm almost afraid to see what it is."

"Let me do it. Why don't you stay in the car?" He opened the driver's door but Sunny was faster.

"I'm coming with you." In the big scheme of things, whatever might have happened in her home didn't really matter. Her only concern was her cat, Miss Priss. Everything else could be fixed or replaced.

"Oh, boy," Landry muttered as he walked up the stairs.

"Here, kitty, kitty," Sunny cajoled, crawling under the bushes. Miss Priss was always on the front porch waiting to greet her. This time she was nowhere in sight.

Giving up her search, she followed Landry up the steps, not quite sure she wanted to discover what he was muttering about.

Even in the gloom Sunny could see the bright red paint slashed across the front of her house.

"Bitch? He's not very original, is he?" Sunny reverted to humor to diffuse a bad situation.

"Sweetheart, don't worry." Landry draped his arm around her shoulders. "I'm calling your uncle." He punched the numbers into his cell.

"I want to find my cat." Sunny walked down the steps and was on her way to the backyard by the time Landry caught up with her.

"The guy might still be here. Wait till I get something out of the car," he instructed, sprinting back to the rental.

Nodding, Sunny sat on the step and watched as Landry searched the vehicle.

Mission accomplished, he jogged back to the porch. "Let's find your kitty. I'm sure she's fine."

Sunny certainly hoped so. If the jerk had so much as touched Miss Priss, she'd hunt him down and neuter him.

But why was she thinking strictly in terms of a male? She personally knew at least one female who was meaner than a junkyard dog. Namely Shelly Orwell, her best friend in junior high, the woman who had always been hot to canoodle Walter. And when everything went to hell with her marriage, Shelly went out of her way to rub it in.

To put it mildly, she was nasty. And then there was Traci Manning. People with bad hair had been known to go ballistic.

"Miss Priss has a bell, so if she moves you can hear her. I put it on because I thought the birds would be safer."

"Okay," Landry said, poking his head around the corner of the detached garage.

"Listen," Sunny paused. "I think I hear her back

toward the fence."

"Miss Priss. Here kitty," she called.

Landry stayed with Sunny while she searched.

Several large camellias created a vegetative barrier to the alley. That's where she found Miss Priss—unhurt, but hissing mad.

"I've got her," Sunny said, cuddling the cat. "It looks like the cops have arrived." Flashing lights illuminated the neighborhood—so much for being subtle.

"Why don't you talk to them while I put her in the house? I don't want her to wander off again." Sunny was already on her way to the back door.

"Sure," Landry agreed, strolling down the drive as if he had the situation well under control.

"I'll be right there," Sunny called out, retrieving her keys and opening the back door. Life was spinning out of control and she didn't know how to stop it.

Someone was threatening her! That was scary, but looking on the bright side, she'd scraped up the courage to ask the sexiest guy in town to move in with her!

In the annals of Sunny McAllister's life, it was a stellar moment!

The good news was that Uncle Dave was taking the vandalism seriously. The bad news was that they'd need a lot more evidence to arrest anyone.

That was when Sunny decided that if she found the vandal before the cops did, she'd nail his hide to the nearest barn door. Rats on the legal system!

Uncle Dave's deputies finally left, the neighbors returned to their respective homes, and Sunny found herself cuddled on the couch with Landry, a bowl of popcorn and Miss Priss.

"I'll paint the front of your house tomorrow." In typical male fashion, Landry had commandeered the remote and was surfing the channels.

"I'm not all that concerned about the paint, although I'm sure the neighbors would like to get rid of the graffiti sooner rather than later. We have kids in the neighborhood." She popped a kernel in her mouth and chewed. "What do you think is happening?"

Landry picked up a handful of popcorn. "I suspect you have an enemy, and your questions have seriously annoyed that person. Can you think of someone who really dislikes you?"

"Everyone has an enemy, Tracy Manning hates my guts, but I don't think she'd resort to graffiti because of a bad hair experience." Sunny thought for a moment but came up with the same answer. "Seriously, I don't I have any real enemies. I'm a nice person."

"I agree." He then proceeded to show her how nice he thought she was. The ball game was soon forgotten.

Thank goodness she'd made a trip to Victoria's Secret. White Wal-Mart undies would not do the trick. Her lacy pink half bra and thong panties, however, were perfect. With that thought in mind, the daredevil in her took over as she pulled off her T-shirt and tossed it over the back of the couch.

Miss Priss hissed her disapproval and skittered

139

Ann DeFee

off toward the kitchen. Landry, on the other hand, was delighted.

"Does that mean what I think it means?"

"Oh, yes," she responded, emphasizing her intent by straddling his hips.

Her newly found confidence created an amazing result—to say the least.

Chapter 23

"Did you hear what happened?" Liza burst into Miss Scarlett's Boudoir the moment Lily opened the door. "I was at the Coffee Klatch and Mrs. Stackhouse cornered me. The old bag was delighted to spread some news about our family."

"What did she tell you?"

"Sunny's house was vandalized last night."

Not only was Mrs. Stackhouse a pain-in-the-butt client of Double Date, she was also one of Sunny's neighbors. Although her gossip was normally a bit suspect, this time she had her facts straight.

"Are you kidding?" Lily plopped on her favorite antique fainting couch. "What kind of vandalism?"

"Mrs. Stackhouse said someone painted *bitch* in red paint all over the front of Sunny's house."

"That old biddy is such a snoop she checks out everyone who drives down the street. Did she see who did it?"

"No. She was at her sister's house in Corpus Christi yesterday." Liza frowned. "The one and only time she could have been helpful and she was out of town."

Liza sat down next to her sister. "I'm afraid we've stirred up a hornet's nest."

"I agree. We need to get Sunny over here for a serious talk." Lily whipped the cell phone out of her blazer pocket. "I want to know what Uncle Dave said."

"Uh-huh."

"Sunny, phone for you," Toolie yelled. "It's Lily."

Would that girl never learn proper telephone manners?

"Hey, Lily. What's up?" It was a rhetorical question; she knew exactly why her cousin was calling.

"Get your cute little butt over here. Liza's here and we want to talk."

"What if I have a perm going? Would you want me to over-process it?"

"Goodness no. Do you? Have a perm in the works, that is."

"No, as a matter of fact my next client isn't due for an hour. I'll be there in a few minutes. I sure hope you guys have come up with something fantastic because I'm fresh out of ideas."

By the time Sunny walked the block to Miss Scarlett's Boudoir, Lily had turned over the closed sign and Liza had broken out the good chocolate.

This had the earmarks of a major summit conference.

"Are you going to share?" Sunny was referring to the box of Godiva Liza had in her lap.

"Sure, here." Her cousin handed her the chocolate. "After my talk with Mrs. Stackhouse I needed some endorphins."

"You talked to Mrs. Stackhouse?" Sunny couldn't suppress a groan.

"Yep. And the current rumor is that Landry's down at the hardware store buying paint," Lily contributed. "Did you by any chance tell him that to be able to cover red paint he had to put a primer on first?"

"What do I know about primer?"

"I'll call him," Lily picked up her phone, but Sunny stopped her.

"He's a big boy, he can figure it out."

"Okay, guys, cut the discussion about paint. We have more important things to talk about. Let's brainstorm." Liza always got down to business. "First, of all, murder isn't common around here, except the time the guys from the retirement community started killing drug dealers—and that was really weird. But in this situation we not only have a homicide, we also have someone—more than likely the murderer—threatening Sunny." She paused to munch on another chocolate. "So why aren't Lily and I getting obnoxious notes?"

Good question; and one that didn't lend itself to an easy answer.

"Maybe it was someone I talked to," Sunny suggested.

"That would mean it was a woman. Or it could be a boyfriend, husband or significant other of one of your clients."

Sunny was pondering the possibility when Liza added a new wrinkle. "I deal with men every day. I should be getting the notes, not you guys."

That was true. The number of men who patronized Miss Scarlett's Boudoir could be counted on one hand; ditto for Sunny's clients. Other than a couple of men who wanted a snazzy haircut, people of the male persuasion were not the mainstay of Double Date.

"Let's assume for a moment that it's someone I contacted," Liza said with a sigh. "That could be just about anyone in the real estate development community. I told Charlie, but he knows what we're doing, and I also spoke to several lawyers, architects and engineers. Someone from that group would be a more likely suspect than anyone you talked to, especially, if we're right about the strip center. So basically we're back to square one. Unless..." She paused. "Unless Walter is our guy. Then threatening Sunny would be more logical. From what I hear, he stands to make a lot of money if this deal goes through. Perhaps he thinks we're about to mess up his plans.

"God, I can't even think that way. We were *married*!" Sunny exclaimed. "I don't want to believe he could murder anyone."

Liza dropped the discussion of Walter and segued to the Hardaways. "Are we excluding Crumpy's family?" she asked. "He has more shirttail relatives than a coon dog had ticks. Someone could have talked to him."

"We aren't excluding the Hardaways. In fact, they're my prime suspects," Lily declared. "Crumpy's flat-out nasty, and the rest of his family is worse."

"Isn't that the truth," Sunny agreed.

"Why do you suppose his grandson tried to rob you?" Liza asked. "You don't keep a lot of cash at the salon."

That question had been bothering Sunny, and she still didn't have an answer.

"I hadn't thought of that," Lily said.

After a pause, Liza continued, "So exactly where are we in our investigation?"

"We know for sure that Bubba Gene didn't do it. He's not capable of hurting anyone,"

"We can come up with all sorts of conjectures,

but that doesn't get us any closer to a suspect. So I suggest we let Uncle Dave do his job." Liza had slipped into her "take charge" mode. "Our plan has successfully generated doubt about Bubba Gene's guilt and that was our primary goal. The unintended result seems to be that Sunny has to be very careful. Don't go anywhere alone."

Although Sunny recognized the wisdom of the suggestion she couldn't resist a bit of sarcasm. "Yes, Mama Liza."

Poor Landry—he didn't know it, but he was about to become her constant companion.

And isn't that nice, Sunny thought with a smirk.

With respect to the efficiency of Port Serenity's grapevine, Landry and Colby decided to stage their investigation out of a neighboring town, so he met his investigators at a Denny's on the freeway.

"I hear we have a problem," Pete commented, digging into his Grand Slam breakfast.

Landry had wisely passed on the cholesterol feast and was nursing a cup of coffee. "Yep, we do. I suppose you've also heard what caused this situation."

Jill grinned. "You have to give it those ladies. They know how to pick a fight."

That would have been fine. In fact, Landry would have applauded the effort if Sunny wasn't involved.

"Do you think you can capitalize on the fact our boy's getting nervous?"

"There's nothing I like better than a jumpy bad guy," Jill said, sporting a huge grin. "I hear you've taken up painting."

Was nothing secret? "I certainly have."

"Did you remember to buy primer?" Jill asked.

"Is that something I need?"

"Positively." Her grin grew even wider. "I'll bet you hire someone to change your oil, don't you?"

"Okay, so I'm not so handy. But I have other talents."

It was obviously the wrong thing to say because both of his investigators started laughing.

"Forget that," Landry shook his head. "Let's get back to business." He'd briefly considered hiring a guard for both the salon and Sunny's house, but considering the *curious* neighbors, he'd quickly aborted that idea. Unless things heated up, he could handle the job.

"Colby will be down next week. We'll get together then. Same time, same place. In the meantime, if you find out anything let me know immediately."

"Okay," Pete said.

"And pay special attention to the Hardaway's."

"They won't be able to sneeze without us knowing it. And since we're gonna be watching so many people, Colby sent two additional investigators as backup."

"Who did he send?"

"Larry and Jason."

"That's great. If you have any questions or anything to report, call my cell."

"Will do, boss," Jill said with a sly smile. "Be sure to buy some primer. If I think of anything else you might need, I'll let you know."

Sheesh. Even his investigators were tuned into

Texas Double Date

the grapevine.

Chapter 24

"Where's Landry?" Toolie asked, popping the top on a cold Dr. Pepper. She didn't wait for an answer before she continued, "Is he going to keep working or do we need to advertise?"

Those were good questions. Sunny didn't know his plans, but she was positive he wouldn't be doing the shampoo job, so yep, they'd better start advertising. "I think we should start looking for a new shampoo *girl*. And this time we're definitely hiring a girl."

"The ladies are gonna be mighty disappointed." That observation came from Raylene.

"And I'll miss all those baked goodies," Toolie said and Penny nodded.

That was true. Until Landry came along, Sunny hadn't realized there were that many brownie recipes.

It was time to come clean about Landry, his real life, the bet, and the fact he'd moved in with her. "I have something I have to tell you that's gonna blow your socks off." She conveniently left out a few details, such as the sizzling hot nature of their relationship, and the fact their cohabitation wasn't simply a matter of safety. That information would be shared on a strictly need-to-know basis.

"So are you going to take him to the historical society party?" Leave it to Raylene to ask the hard question.

"With Bubba Gene and everything that's been going on, I haven't given it a thought."

"Bubba Gene would be upset if you gave up a fancy party because of him. And girlie, the shindig is this Saturday. I know for a fact you sent them a 'yes' RSVP, a long time ago."

Sunny vaguely remembered putting that in the mail. Aunt Anna Belle was the current Historical Society president, which meant that if Sunny wanted to remain a family member in good standing, she'd be going to the party.

"Should I take Landry?" It was a rhetorical question. Of course she'd invite him.

"Yes," Raylene and Toolie yelled in unison.

"Even if this all started because of a bet?"

"Especially considering what he did to win the bet. From what you said, if he doesn't go to the party he loses. You don't want that to happen, do you?" Toolie asked.

"No, I don't." Her family would wholeheartedly approve of her date, especially Anna Belle and Eugenie. They had a soft spot when it came to Landry Valliere.

Join the club. What red-blooded American girl wouldn't find him alluring? The man was charm personified, and at least this time they wouldn't have to raid the Haberdashery for something appropriate to wear.

"I suppose we can use it as his coming-out party. It will be our chance to introduce him to society."

"Right on," Raylene agreed. "How about that, Landry's gonna be Port Serenity's newest debutante."

Sunny had just put her client under the dryer when she heard an argument up front. Not again! When she spied the source of the altercation, her stomach did a somersault. It was Traci Manning, aka Bridezilla, and her hair was even worse than before. Fortunately, she hadn't been back since the wedding day hair fiasco.

"Hi Traci." Sunny decided to go for being friendly.

"Don't you *hi Traci* me, you bitch," she yelled. Spittle flew all over the counter. "You've ruined my life. My husband can barely look at me without laughing. I couldn't face another trip to a beauty salon, so I decided to fix it myself, "she wailed as she lifted a strand of ruined hair.

Sunny was almost knocked over by the fumes. Big uh-oh! Traci was not only mad, she was plastered. She hoped violence could be avoided, but when it came to an irate customer nothing was a certainty.

"Traci, why don't you come on back with me? We'll see what we can do to fix it," Sunny said, steering the woman toward the rear of the salon. As they passed Raylene, she mimed a phone call, and mouthed "if necessary."

Raylene nodded, surreptitiously holding up her cell.

Sunny pushed her unwilling client into the chair and managed to get a cape around her neck. Lord in heaven, what had happened? If she got this stuff looking like real hair again, it was going to be a miracle.

"Did you try to color it yourself?"

Traci hiccupped. "Yeah, that purple stuff sucked."

"Raylene, would you come here a minute? I need another opinion."

Raylene strolled over and studied Traci's head from every angle. Then she called Toolie.

Toolie's advice was succinct. "Cut it all off. There's not much you can do for it now."

Traci's wail—one that incidentally could have been heard in the next county—left no doubt as to how she felt about the suggestion.

It took almost an hour of cutting and conditioning before Traci was presentable. The style wasn't great—to say the least—but, it was acceptable and that was a huge improvement.

"Do you think she appreciates what we did?" Toolie asked as they watched Traci slam the door.

"Nope. We're convenient scapegoats for everything that's going wrong in her life," Sunny said. "Why don't you guys go on home? I'll clean up. I think Landry might be coming by in a little bit."

"I'm out of here," Raylene said, heading for the front door. Toolie was a half-step behind her.

Landry parked in the small gravel lot behind Double Date. His plan was to take Sunny out for a romantic dinner, complete with candles, wine, flowers and cuisine that didn't come out of a sack. The courting was about to commence.

It was almost six o'clock, so all the clients should be gone. At that time of the afternoon Sunny was usually in her office doing paperwork. Landry fingered the velvet petals of the two dozen pink roses he'd picked up at the florist.

Although he wasn't sure how things would eventually work out, he knew with certainty that he was in love. If it meant doing a complete one-eighty in his professional life, so be it. Defending the dregs of New

151

Orleans society had lost its appeal, and money wasn't an issue.

A strange noise jerked his thoughts back to the present. What was that? Another crackling sound came from inside the shop, and Landry was out of the car in a flash.

Hopefully Sunny hadn't secured the alarm. Landry yanked the door open and caught a whiff of smoke.

Where was the fire?

He frantically scanned the storeroom to determine the origin of the flames and almost immediately spotted a wisp coming from under the bathroom door. Where was that darned fire extinguisher?

"Sunny, Sunny," he yelled. "Call 911. We have a fire." He hoped she could hear him. She sometimes did her computer work with the headphones on and the music cranked up. When she was tuned in, elephants could stomp through the shop and she wouldn't hear them.

Dredging up all the information he'd ever learned during Fire Prevention Week, Landry gingerly touched the door. Releasing a firestorm would not be a good thing.

Sunny squealed, making an appearance in the connecting doorway. "Fire! Where?"

"The bathroom. Call 911," Landry instructed without turning.

The door was fairly cool to the touch. That indicated the fire hadn't taken control; however, he didn't have the luxury of waiting for the fire trucks.

Landry relied on good common sense as he carefully opened the entrance, ready to slam it and get out of the building if necessary.

Whew! The flames were confined to a pile of paper in the trash can. And unless mice were now playing with matches, an arsonist had left his calling card. Fortunately the firebug wasn't a professional, but fire was fire. And any conflagration had the potential to kill.

Landry put those dire thoughts on hold. First things first, extinguish the flames; then find the son of a gun who started it. Lord pity the guy if Landry got his hands on him.

By the time the authorities arrived, he had smothered the fire. However, the smoldering garbage was causing a significant amount of residual smoke.

Sunny was trying her best not to kick, scream or generally pitch a hissy. Threatening notes were bad enough, but this time some idiot had attacked her salon. She was *not* amused; in fact, she was close to being homicidal. Double Date was her baby and she was a mama grizzly.

Chapter 25

Although the front part of the salon wasn't impacted, smoke damage made business as usual impossible.

Sunny grumbled and groused, and eventually realized all the griping in the world wouldn't remedy a thing. So she calmed down, called the repair people, locked the door and decided to worry about the details later. Insurance would cover the damage, and all things considered, she could use a couple of days off. Fortunately the grooming salon had been spared most of the damage and Penny could continue operating.

"Let's go home and get cleaned up. I smell like a bonfire." Landry pulled the hem of his shirt up to his nose.

"Uh-huh," Sunny agreed. That man had world-class abs. But how could she be thinking about sex when an arsonist had wreaked havoc on her business? It had to be a delayed reaction to stress, or one of those "let's go party 'cause I almost got hit by a bus" kind of things.

"Before we do anything else I have to call Raylene and Toolie to let them know what happened. And if I don't tell my family about the fire, I'll be disowned," she said with a half-grin. "Then I need to reschedule the next couple of day's appointments."

"I'll help." He pulled his cell phone out of his pocket and steered her toward his car.

Darn it—she'd weathered the crisis of the fire and graciously made it through the fire marshal's questions, but the bouquet of roses did her in. One look at the beautiful pink flowers and the dam of tears burst.

Some guys ran at the first sight of a female crying. Others reverted to sarcasm. Landry, however, proved to be a trooper.

"Don't worry. Things will work out." He pulled her into his arms and let her use his shirt as a towel.

With him, there wasn't any of that awkward back-patting. Walter had been especially uncomfortable with emotional displays, but he'd been embarrassed about almost everything she did.

Sunny wiped her nose on her sleeve and gave a final sigh. Miss Alicia, the etiquette guru, would have had a fit, but hey, Sunny had more important things on her mind.

"A shower sounds like heaven," she winked at her best guy. "Or maybe a leisurely soak. Would you like to share?"

"Absolutely!" Landry hit the gas pedal like a rookie NASCAR driver.

Sunny was expecting a nice long bath for two, a romantic dinner and some good lovin'. But somewhere between Point A and Point B, Landry had decided on another agenda and being a typical male, he hadn't bothered to share. He was in and out of the shower so fast he barely got the tiles wet, and off he went with a phone stuck to his ear.

Well, at least she was clean and her hair didn't smell like the inside of a barbecue, Sunny thought as she marched into the kitchen. Not much solace when she'd had an erotic agenda in mind.

The refrigerator door barely withstood the assault as she jerked it open. It was wine time. She popped out the cork and poured a liberal dollop into a plastic Big Gulp cup.

Sunny didn't get miffed often, but when she did, it was a sight to behold. The cousins claimed she was downright scary. They called it her Brunhilda mood. She took another slurp and slammed the cabinet door.

He was the last guy on the planet she'd ask to the big party. No way, no how!

Landry pumped a fist in the air. Going away for the weekend was a stroke of genius, and he hadn't wasted time in implementing his great idea. In a matter of minutes he'd score a reservation at an exclusive resort in the Texas Hill Country. Sunny was due for some pampering, and he was looking forward to a weekend of indulging her.

Landry was flushed with success. He couldn't wait to give her the good news and receive a kiss as his reward. "Hey, peaches—" He never got the chance to complete his sentence.

"Don't peaches me!"

Uh-oh. He was in a mess of trouble and he didn't have a clue what he'd done. It was a worst-case scenario for a guy.

"I, uh—"

Sunny interrupted him, grabbing her cordless phone. "I'm calling for pizza."

She didn't bother to ask whether he liked pepperoni or pineapple. That wasn't a good sign, and her glittery green eyes were definitely not an encouraging omen. He'd heard about Brunhilda from the cousins, but up to that point he hadn't actually met her. And he wasn't sure he wanted to make her acquaintance now.

Despite all odds, and being the brave guy he was, Landry marched into the fray. On the silver screen cowards never got the girl. And, by gosh, he planned to snag this heroine. A sneak attack was in order—complete with kissing, and nuzzling, and whatever came next.

"I'm—"

He didn't give her a chance to complete her thought.

"Shh," he demanded, slanting his lips over hers, then he moved down her neck toward his ultimate destination.

When they finally came up for air he went on the offensive. "I'm sorry."

When in doubt, an apology was always in order. It was a lesson he'd learned early in his dating experience, and if past history held, it had about a fifty-fifty success rate.

"Hmm," she murmured, pulling him down for another kiss.

That was good. Actually it was fantastic. Forgiveness *was* in his future, and hopefully there'd be some R-rated adventures, too.

A couple of hours later, they took a water-saving shower for two. "I have a great idea," he ventured, running his fingers through her wet strands of hair.

"Uh-huh."

"I've made reservations for us to spend a couple of days at the Willow Tree Resort."

"You've done what?" She backed up a step.

Landry garnered all his powers of persuasion. "Since you can't open the salon and you've made arrangements for the cleanup and repair, I thought you'd like to get away for a little while. How does a massage, a canoe ride in the moonlight, and some quality time with me sound?" Landry had resorted to cajoling and he was more than willing to beg if necessary.

"It sounds good. Where's the Willow Tree?"

"It's in the Hill Country."

"That sounds terribly tempting."

"Yes, ma'am." He punctuated his agreement with a long, slow kiss.

"And I'm sure Liza will be glad to keep Miss Priss," she muttered. "So kiss me again."

How could Landry resist? He was, after all, a red-blooded American male in a very small shower enclosure with an incredibly delectable female. And he loved her and planned to spend the rest of his life with her.

Chapter 26

The next day they got a late start, so it was early afternoon before they reached the Willow Tree.

"This is fantastic!" Sunny exclaimed, surveying the grounds of the resort. It was a delightful surprise. The groupings of limestone cottages were connected by tropical vegetation and walkways lined with live oak trees.

The brochure she picked up at the registration desk indicated that the main hotel was originally a farm house built by one of the early German immigrants in the early 1840's. However, time and economic spirals, had taken its toll until an insightful entrepreneur bought the property for a song and created the Willow Tree Resort.

"It is nice, isn't it," Landry agreed, surrendering his car keys for valet parking. "My incredibly efficient assistant found it on the internet and booked it for us."

"Thank her, or him, for being so resourceful," Sunny said with a smile. She was savoring the array of flowers and the addictively sweet scent of honeysuckle. And while she didn't verbalize it, Sunny thanked her lucky stars for having a thoughtful guy like Landry in her life. The survivor of a failed marriage, she knew all too well that not many men were cut from that cloth.

Landry glanced at the packet the desk clerk handed him. "It looks like we're staying in the Cottonwood Cottage. Sounds nice, doesn't it?"

"Mm-hmm." Sunny was so engrossed in checking out the surroundings, she almost didn't answer. The place was romance at its best, and they

Ann DeFee

hadn't scratched the surface of possibilities.

Sunny had needed a vacation for a long time, but for a variety of reasons she hadn't taken the time. Perhaps she'd simply been waiting for Landry.

Cottonwood Cottage was the essence of daydreams. It was Texas architecture at its best with a facade of a pale cream limestone and a metal roof.

"Oh my," Sunny murmured, surveying the interior of the cottage. "It's simply beautiful." Antiques, a wood burning fireplace, tall ceilings and fresh flowers created a cozy, but elegant, ambiance.

Landry wandered off toward the bedroom. The man was as transparent as a piece of Saran Wrap.

Sunny followed him. Okay, she'd admit it. She had the same idea.

The living room was lovely, but the bedroom exceeded all expectations. The antique sleigh bed was fit for a princess.

"What do you think about checking out the accommodations?" Landry asked, putting his arms around her and nudging her toward the edge of the mattress.

He didn't have to ask twice. Sunny fell into the middle of a pile of pillows.

"The bellboy will be here in a few minutes," she reminded him as he removed his belt and pulled down the zipper of his trousers.

"Oops, I forgot." Landry frowned as he restored his clothing and strolled toward the front of the cottage, not a minute too soon.

The situation with the suitcases settled, they

could get down to the fun stuff. Could they ever!

Sunny ran her fingers through his chest hair, massaging his rock-hard abs in the process. That felt so good she could do it all night, and she was absolutely positive he wouldn't object.

"If you keep that up, we'll miss dinner." He captured her hand and kissed her palm.

"Dinner, bed, dinner, kissing. Do I really have to make a choice?" At that point, Sunny's stomach expressed an opinion.

"That settles it. We're heading to the dining room. Later, I suggest we check out the claw-footed tub."

"Sounds like a plan." Her agreement was punctuated by another tummy rumble.

"Are you enjoying yourself?" Landry asked toward the end of a scrumptious meal.

"Of course." Sunny couldn't keep the smile off her face. She was having a romantic adventure with the man of her dreams—the nasty stuff back home was on the back burner. There was, however, the tiny problem that they'd never discussed significant things like finances, and even more important, their relationship. As far as she was concerned, the love thing was easy. She was head over heels crazy about him.

The finances were another matter entirely. The menu prices at this place were enough to make your eyes water, and God only knew what he was paying for the room. Could he really afford it? He was an attorney, but that didn't necessarily mean he was flush with money. Some of the lawyers she knew were barely making ends meet.

So Sunny did what she thought was the sensible thing and suggested they go Dutch treat. That was met with a resounding *no way*. Stubborn man! When he mentioned a day at the Spa, Sunny countered with the option of a hike. She pointed out that there were also some free adventures they didn't have to leave the cottage to enjoy.

"Let's skip dessert and go back to the room. I'm feeling like a bath," she said with a grin.

Before she could blink an eye, Landry hailed the waiter and paid their check.

Lord, you had to love an enthusiastic man—especially one with slow hands and a passionate heart.

Chapter 27

Landry had muscles on muscles, Sunny thought, as she watched him row. Sure, she could take a turn with the paddles, but why spoil the view. As a surprise he'd ordered a gourmet basket for them to enjoy at the picnic area across the lake.

"Are you planning to help?" he asked, with the quirk of a smile.

"And ruin the macho thing?"

"You're right." He gave her a wink and a grin. "Sit back and relax."

He didn't have to ask her twice. The past couple of weeks had been mentally exhausting. Plus, they hadn't had much sleep last night, and the glide of the boat was so peaceful. With the warm sun on her face and the country sounds in the background, Sunny drifted off.

Suddenly her peaceful interlude was interrupted by a strange noise that ripped through the quiet. Landry shouted an expletive as the canoe tipped over.

Not another snake! Sunny slowly drifted toward the bottom of the pond. Her brain and muscles weren't on the same page.

Fortunately, Landry had his act together and pulled her to the surface. "Someone's shooting at us. Swim underwater as far as you can. Don't come up until you absolutely have to, and go in that direction." He pointed toward the dock behind their cottage.

He didn't have to ask her twice. This was by far worse than a threatening note, or even a snake.

"You're coming, aren't you?" she squealed.

"Right behind you."

Another shot rang out as the pair ducked under water.

This was getting damned old. She was not *ever* getting in a canoe again!

One of the ground maintenance people witnessed the incident and reported it to his superiors. Their 911 call prompted an emergency response, and within thirty minutes the cottage was swarming with cops and resort management. Less than an hour later investigators from Texas Department of Public Safety arrived.

Sunny and Landry had changed clothes and were sitting together on the couch. He was holding her hand making her feel somewhat better, not top of the morning, but better.

"What do you bet a team of lawyers is on its way from Austin," Landry muttered as he squeezed her fingers.

That was a no-brainer. Of course the attorneys were making a mad dash to the Willow Tree. Having guests shot at while on resort property was a huge liability issue. But a lawsuit was the last thing on Sunny's mind. All she wanted to do was get home and slam the door—blocking out the rest of the world.

"The minute we're through giving the investigator our statements we're leaving," Landry informed the manager, interrupting his litany of innocent possibilities ranging from errant hunters to firecrackers.

The explanations were a crock. Someone had advanced from fear tactics to attempted murder, and that scared Sunny right down to the tips of her pink-painted toenails.

"The minute we hit the Port Serenity city limits, I'm heading over to talk to Dave. This has gone way too far," Landry declared, not taking his eyes off her.

Amen to that. "I'll call him and tell him we're on our way. Knowing him, by the time we hit the city limits, he'll be sitting in front of my house with the lights flashing."

That was exactly what Landry was counting on. He'd almost swallowed his tongue when he'd realized the noise was gunfire, and it was aimed at them.

Hell—that would have rattled anyone.

The ride home was ominously silent. Sunny had shut down—no tears, no ranting, nothing. It was so un-Sunny-ish that it threw Landry for a loop. How did he handle the silent waif huddled in the passenger seat?

That became the least of his problems when her cell phone rang.

"It says pay phone on the caller ID," she muttered, the color leaching from her face.

Landry moved to the side of the road and cut the engine. "Answer and hold it up so I can hear, too."

The voice was electronically altered, so it was impossible to discern whether it was male or female. The message, though, was loud and clear.

"I told you to stop meddling and you just kept at it. The shot was a warning—the next time I won't miss."

Sunny hit the end icon. "That makes me absolutely furious!"

Landry was almost glad to see her get agitated; it was much better than melancholy.

"I want you to stay away from me," she declared,

turning her face toward the window.

"What?"

"Stay. Away. From. Me. Is that clear enough?"

Landry resisted a chuckle. This tiny Peter Pan wanted to protect him—but being the smart guy he was—he didn't crack a grin.

"Let's not discuss that. At least not until we talk to Dave."

She shot him a grim look. Stubborn was her middle name. Well, that was too bad. He'd had the Dixie Mafia on his tail and they hadn't intimidated him. Sunny didn't stand a chance.

Chapter 28

"Tell me exactly what happened." Sheriff Dave was sitting on Sunny's couch with a notebook in one hand and a cup of coffee in the other. In some ways it felt like an ordinary visit; however, when Uncle Dave visited he usually ditched the gun and uniform. This time he was in full regalia. Not only that, he had on his cop face.

Landry glanced in her direction. "Sunny and I went to the Hill Country for a little getaway. We hadn't been at the resort more than a day when someone took a potshot at us. We were out in a canoe when it happened."

"Are you sure it wasn't a hunter with bad aim?"

"Positive. The DPS guys didn't think so, either."

"Can't argue with the big boys," Dave admitted. "Did you get a look at the guy?"

"No. I was busy rowing, and Sunny was napping. I can give you the name of the person in charge of the investigation. The folks at the resort are very nervous, so I suspect a thorough search of the area was done."

"You two don't have good luck with boats, do you?" Dave asked with a chuckle. "I'll wager those hotel folks are about to hack up a fur ball worrying about litigation."

"And I'm not about to disabuse them of the idea. At least, not until we get some answers. But that's not the worst of it. Sunny got a threatening phone call on our way home."

"What did the caller say," Sheriff Dave

demanded. At that point he was all business.

Landry relayed the conversation verbatim.

"Well, damn," Dave exclaimed, and then he paused for a moment before continuing. "I have an idea, but I'll need Sunny's help to pull it off."

"I'm willing to do anything you want." That was her first contribution to the conversation.

"Okay, here it is. This garbage started when you girls tapped the rumor mill. I think you should talk to Miss Laverne Hightower and see what she knows." Dave chuckled. "Right now I'm not her favorite person, or I'd do it."

Sunny chewed on her bottom lip, then smiled. "That's a great idea. And you're absolutely correct. She *wouldn't* let you in the house. I heard she had her tail feathers all fluffed up when you towed her car.

"What else could I do? She left it in a loading zone for three days."

Landry was at a loss. Who were they talking about? Then he remembered the octogenarian from the salon. It sometimes felt as if the people in Port Serenity spoke a foreign language.

Sunny took pity on him. "Miss Laverne is the one who identified Crumpy's grandson after our robbery. She knows everything that happens in this town. In fact, she has dirt on almost everyone in the county. And no one can figure out how she does it, because other than coming to the salon and going to church, she's a hermit. I do her hair but she still scares me."

"Don't worry, I'll go with you," Landry said. "I don't think we have much choice."

Sunny pulled out her cell, and while she was talking, to Miss Hightower, Landry broached another subject.

"Dave, I think you should have another long talk with Bubba Gene," Landry suggested. "Maybe if you ask some different questions he might dredge up something new."

"It's worth a shot," Dave agreed. "I've talked to him myself, and my detectives have questioned him, but perhaps we weren't approaching him the right way."

"Okay guys, she's expecting us in an hour, and she's really excited about Landry coming."

"I can't wait," Landry said with a wry smile.

"You need to learn to control that sarcasm." Sunny admonished him with a giggle. The poor guy looked about as eager as a kid trudging to the principal's office.

Sunny opened the creaky gate of the picket fence and walked up a path overgrown with vines and trailing roses. I don't know if you remember, but Miss Laverne is somewhat eccentric."

"That's nothing unusual. Just about everyone in this town is eccentric."

She ignored his comment as she tapped on the front door of the gingerbread Victorian. Landry picked at a strip of peeling paint on the doorjamb.

"Stop that," Sunny demanded, tapping his hand.

"Hi, there, Miss Laverne. You remember Landry from the salon. He washed your hair."

"Of course I remember him. I might be old as the hills, but I'm not addled. Come on in. I've made some fresh lemonade." Laverne opened the screen door and ushered her visitors inside. In a move worthy of a cotillion queen, Laverne grabbed Landry's arm and batted her eyelashes.

Sunny couldn't resist an eye roll as she followed Landry and Miss Laverne into the house. She felt like a third wheel on a really bad date.

There were just some things you didn't rush, and Texas hospitality was at the top of the list. So, they spent an hour snacking on lemonade and sugar cookies. Finally Sunny worked

up the nerve to ask the big question.

"There's something really important we need to find out."

"What is it?"

"It's about Aunt Hallie's murder."

"Poor woman, things like that shouldn't happen around here. Whoever did it needs to be strung up. Don't know why they don't do public hangings anymore. That would put a halt to crime."

"Yes, ma'am," Sunny murmured, leaning forward to ensure she had the older woman's attention. "We're trying to find out if anyone saw or heard anything at Aunt Hallie's that day, and for whatever reason they haven't come forward."

Laverne rested her chin on her hand. "Let me see, hmm. Wonder what Stanley Cook knows? Not that the old coot remembers his own name most of the time," she muttered to herself. "He's Aunt Hallie's back-alley neighbor."

Sunny glanced at Landry. She could tell he was

trying to stifle a grin. Who could blame him? This wasn't exactly a Sherlock Holmes moment.

"By gosh, I think he *is* the guy we need to talk to. Let me give him a buzz just to make sure I'm right." Laverne searched through the pile of papers and magazines on the coffee table in an attempt to find her phone.

"Hey, there, Stanley. Welcome home. How's Miss Maude doing?" There was a long silence before she spoke again. "You tell that sweet wife of yours to keep her feet elevated and get lots of sleep. She'll be fit as a fiddle before you know it. Now, I've got a question, and think real hard before you answer. The day you and Maude left for Colorado, did you see anyone visit Aunt Hallie?"

There was another long silence. "Is that right?"

Sunny's nerve endings were jumping with curiosity.

"Do tell," Miss Laverne said before lapsing into another long silence.

So *that* was how she gleaned her information. She was a good listener. It was a lesson a lot of people should learn.

After a short discussion of the merits of mayonnaise versus Miracle Whip, Miss Laverne finally got off the phone.

"I personally like Miracle Whip," Sunny offered, not that she was asked, or that it was relevant.

"Me, too," Miss Laverne agreed. "Stanley can go off on the strangest tangents, but that's neither here nor there. He and his wife were at their cabin up in the Rockies. They just got back yesterday."

"Miss Laverne, what did he notice?" Sunny asked, trying to keep her on task.

"Let's see. He told me that he saw Walter go in her back door that day. He's pretty sure about the date because they were packing to leave. He heard about Hallie getting killed, but until I tweaked his memory, he'd forgotten about seeing Walter. Poor man, he's been having a few senior moments lately, but I guess that's understandable—he has his hands full with Maude. She's not in good health."

"Walter? Are you talking about my ex-husband, Walter?"

"One and the same."

Walter? No way! He couldn't be a murderer, could he? There had to be a logical reason for his visit to Aunt Hallie. But what? She wasn't one of his drinking buddies.

She did, however, own a valuable piece of property. And Walter had a vested interest in making sure that the real estate project went forward. Jeeze, oh jeeze, oh man! Not Walter! Not the man she'd pledged to love forever. Did that make her the worst judge of character on the planet?

Sunny knew that every one of those thoughts flitted across her face because when she glanced at Landry, he was frowning.

"I think we should make another visit to the sheriff," he suggested.

Damned straight, and the Texas Department of Public Safety the Texas Rangers, and the FBI, and the CIA… Okay, slow down, girl. Deep breath…one, two, three, another deep breath.

"You're right." Sunny agreed, then gave Miss Laverne a hug.

"As distressing as this news is, I appreciate it. Hopefully, we can clear Bubba Gene's name."

The elderly woman reciprocated with a squeeze. "I've always liked that boy. His mother was a real lady, one of the best."

The Sheriff's Office had seen better days. The last remodel had to have been part of the Depression Era make-work program. It looked more like a dungeon than a cop shop, Sunny thought as they made their way through a rabbit warren of small offices and even more diminutive cubicles.

"Hey, sweetie. Tell me you have good news." Dave said, embracing Sunny.

"Landry, good to see you." The two men shook hands. "Have a seat. I'm hopin' you have something good to tell me." Dave indicated two well-worn leather chairs in front of his desk.

"I don't know that I'd call it good," Sunny said with a sigh. "But we did go over to Miss Laverne's house."

Dave propped his elbows on his desk. "What did you find out?"

"We, uh, she, uh…"

Landry took over the explanation. "She called Stanley Cook, one of Hallie's neighbors. He's been out of town since before the body was discovered, but he said he was packing the car that day and remembers seeing Walter Harrington go into the house."

"Damn. After the murder we tried to find the Cooks to interview them, but they'd already left for their mountain cabin and they don't have a phone up there. I didn't know they were back. Why didn't Stanley call me?"

"I asked that exact question," Landry said. "According to Miss Laverne, he simply didn't make the connection, at least not until she jogged his memory."

"Son of a gun!" Dave exclaimed with a sheepish expression. "I hate to say it, but I never liked Walter. He's too slick for my taste."

Dave's observation merited applause. Too bad Sunny hadn't noticed Walter's obvious deficiency before she'd said "I do."

Dave picked up the phone and hit some numbers. "Gerald, would you come in here, please. There's something I want you to hear." The sheriff hung up and pushed his chair away from the desk. "Gerald's my best detective, so I want him involved. How about I get you something cold to drink? We might be here a while."

Truer words were never spoken. The order of the day was a brainstorming session about scrutinizing one of the town's leading citizens without creating too much heartburn.

Fortunately, the police had obtained some DNA from the scene. So now their problem was how to snooker Walter into making a donation. There were two options: following him around to see if he discarded anything useful, or having Sunny invite him to her house.

"No way," Landry objected.

"Wait," Sunny said, putting her hand on his arm.

"I think it'll work. I found some of his old books and stuff in the attic. I was going to throw everything away but I could ask him to come over and pick it up." She grinned. "It'll work, I know it will."

"If you're dead set on doing this, I plan to be in the other room." Landry put his arms across his chest.

"My deputies and I will be outside just in case something goes wrong," Dave assured her.

"No kidding! I don't want to be alone with a murderer. Not that I haven't been alone with him before. A lot, in fact." Sunny frowned, thinking about her intimate relationship with a possible felon.

Why did she have such abominable taste in men? She glanced at Landry. Well, at least her taste had improved—considerably.

Chapter 29

Although Sunny's attic was stifling, she attacked the chore of boxing Walter's possessions with the passion of a dervish. She'd spent too many years feeling sorry for him.

Before she knew it, she had three boxes of knickknacks, books and old clothes stacked by the front door. She'd prefer to toss the crap out to the curb, but that wouldn't provide the saliva sample they needed. So, like it or not, she was about to play hostess.

"How are you doing?" Landry asked, kissing her neck.

He'd been such a trooper, braving the attic and supplying the muscle power. "Not bad. I want to get this over with."

"I can't blame you. Remember, I'll be in the kitchen, so don't let him go in there."

That wouldn't be a problem. In all the years they'd been married the only time Walter entered the kitchen was to snag a beer.

"Here he comes." Sunny didn't panic often, but wow, her heart was beating a mile a minute.

"Don't worry. If things get dicey, scream and I'll come running," Landry assured her before disappearing through the door, and not a minute too soon. The doorbell rang.

Showtime.

"Walter, come in." She opened the screen door.

"Looks like you're trying to get rid of me again," her ex said, eyeing the pile of boxes.

"Although we're divorced, we should try to be

civil," Sunny responded. "Would you like some iced tea?" She'd rather serve him strychnine, but it was time to think like Nancy Drew.

Walter wandered into the living room, fingering everything in sight.

Get your hands off my things.

"I suppose I could stay around for a cold drink."

"Fine, I'll get it." Sunny scampered off to the kitchen. The minute he left, she planned to take a long, hot shower. Lord in heaven, she felt dirty.

Landry put his arms around her, brushing her mouth with a kiss. "You're doing fine. Take a deep breath and think calming thoughts."

"You mean like killing him?"

"That works."

To facilitate their evidence gathering, Sunny had prepared a tray with two glasses and a pitcher. No cookies, no treats, absolutely nothing that would delay Walter's departure. All she wanted to do was obtain some spit. Then she'd kick his worthless behind out the door.

"We have it!" she exclaimed. After Walter left, Sunny carefully poured out the remainder of the tea and placed his glass in a Ziploc bag. She proudly displayed her prize to Dave and his detective. "How long will it take to process?"

"It'll be at least a week, probably more like two. And that's putting a rush on it. We have to send it to Austin," Gerald told her.

"Seriously?" That wasn't the way it worked on TV. "So you can't do anything until you get some evidence, huh?"

"That's our process. We're eager to close this case, too. So don't worry," Dave reassured her.

Somehow that seemed easier said than done.

Life slowly resumed its normal cadence as Landry tried to decide the best way to approach Bubba Gene. Although he wanted Walter to be guilty, something was out of kilter, and he intended to find out what it was. But he wasn't ready to tell Sunny about his plan, at least not yet.

"Hey, Bubba Gene. Would you like to go with me to the Temptee Freeze? I'll treat you to a milk shake."

"That'd be right nice. I thank ya very much. Let me put my mop away and wash my hands. Mama always told me to clean my hands before I ate anything. Do you do that?" Bubba asked.

"I certainly do," Landry agreed.

Landry waited until his new friend had almost finished his strawberry milkshake before he broached the subject.

"Can you tell me what happened to Aunt Hallie?" Landry was experienced in questioning reluctant witness; however, in this situation he had to be extra careful.

Bubba Gene ducked his head and tied a knot in the straw.

"Cross my heart, I promise I won't say anything."

"Mr. Landry, I'm in bad trouble, aren't I?"

"Perhaps not. We'll have to see how things go," Landry responded as honestly as he could.

Bubba Gene was quiet for such a long time, Landry was afraid he had clammed up.

"That day I was cuttin' grass, you know like I always do on Saturdays before I go to the movies." He paused and looked at Landry. "Do you like Elsa?"

"Yes, I do." Landry tried to redirect the conversation. "Now back to that day at Aunt Hallie's place."

"I heard this racket, and then people were yelling. So I thought I should go see what was happenin'. I was afraid Aunt

Hallie was in trouble. Would you get me another milkshake?"

"Sure. What flavor?"

"Chocolate."

"I'll be right back." This was going to take patience, but Landry wasn't about to quit.

Bubba Gene finished the second shake but remained silent. Landry knew a stall when he saw one.

"So back to Aunt Hallie, what happened next?"

Bubba Gene picked at the edge of his paper cup. "I went into the kitchen, and there she was, all bloody and everything. I didn't do it, really I didn't." A single tear ran down his cheek.

"I know."

"Really, you don't think I did somethin' bad?" There was hope in his voice.

"No, I don't think you did anything bad."

Landry's assurance was enough incentive for Bubba Gene to continue. "I squatted down next to her and tried to keep all that blood from coming out, but I

179

couldn't, it just kept comin' and comin'. Then the maid came in and started screaming. I tried to get her to help, but she yelled louder. She was mad at me. I thought about runnin' but I couldn't leave Aunt Hallie."

"Did you see who was in the kitchen with her?"

"Nope, can we go back to Miss Sunny's now?"

Landry realized that was all the information he was going to get from Bubba Gene, but he had to ask the final question. "Did you see Mr. Walter Harrington?"

"Oh, no, he did come by that day, but I talked to Aunt Hallie after he left."

Well, damn!

Chapter 30

While Bubba Gene and Landry were busy blowing Sunny's theory of the murder out of the water, she was pondering the historical society party. At dinner the night before she'd asked Landry if he still wanted to attend. Not surprisingly, he had answered her with a kiss.

Damn—she loved the way that man thought.

Then she remembered the bet—the wager that had brought him into her life. That dirty dog wanted to go so he could win. After she'd huffed and puffed, and generally acted like a brat, Landry had the audacity to laugh.

"What did you buy?" Raylene took the shopping bag out of Sunny's hands. "My curiosity is killing me."

"Me, too." Toolie was jumping up and down, waiting for Sunny to display her purchase.

After she'd succumbed to Landry's powers of persuasion, Sunny's next thought was typically female; what was she going to wear? Most of her wardrobe ran toward jeans and T-shirts, with a couple of skirts and blouses thrown in for baby showers and Tupperware parties, and there was also the dress she wore to the wedding.

Against her better judgment, Sunny went on a pilgrimage to buy something pretty. The party was an event she'd always managed to avoid, so she was clueless about the appropriate attire.

"What do you think?" She pulled a dress from a glossy shopping bag. The gauzy fabric looked like an

Impressionist painting with a palette of pale pink swirling toward a soft rose.

The saleswoman had assured her it was the perfect outfit. But she'd been working on a commission. Now Sunny was about to get the truth from a couple of ladies who were known for being painfully honest.

"That's beautiful," Toolie murmured.

"Oh, honey. You're gonna knock his socks off," Raylene gushed. "It's a dress made for royalty."

That was exactly what Sunny wanted to hear. "You're sure it's okay?"

Raylene held it up to Sunny. "This little number is more than okay. It has the Raylene Yarborough stamp of approval. And we're gonna come over to help you get dressed."

"Tell you what, I'll bring my clothes to the salon and you guys can work your miracle." Sunny wanted Landry's eyes to bug out when he saw her.

Raylene gave her one of those "what are you up to?" looks before she smiled. Yep, her friend wasn't fooled.

The day of the party dawned clear and gorgeous. It was seasonably warm, but not stifling, and even better; there wasn't a thunderstorm in sight. Too bad Sunny wasn't feeling quite as dazzling. At the last minute, she'd realized she'd rather go to a tractor pull than get all gussied up and hang out in someone's backyard, regardless of their horticultural prowess.

"You're looking gorgeous. Monet couldn't have done it better," Landry said, distributing soft kisses up and down her collarbone. "I love you," he whispered.

Whew! That was the exact reaction Sunny was going for. It was time to buy a closetful of frilly dresses.

"You look pretty good yourself." She couldn't get past how handsome her date was in his exquisitely tailored suit and red silk tie.

"Shall we go?"

"I suppose we have to. Although I can think of a couple of other things we could do," Sunny said with a wink.

"Don't tempt me. Anna Belle would be mad if we were a no-show."

"Yeah," Sunny agreed, somewhat reluctantly.

Landry had decided to hold off on telling anyone about his conversation with Bubba Gene, especially Sunny. He wasn't sure how she would react. A couple of days wouldn't hurt, and he really didn't want to ruin the party.

"How are my two favorite people?" Anna Belle asked, giving Sunny a hug. "Are you having fun?"

"Of course." Sunny smiled at her aunt. If Landry hadn't been privy to her muttering, *he* would have thought she was enjoying herself.

"Miss Anna Belle, this is wonderful. You've outdone yourself. Shall we have a toast?" Landry held up his champagne flute. "To the prettiest women in town."

Anna Belle blushed as she raised her glass. "You're right about Sunny being beautiful."

"You're both gorgeous."

Anna Belle gave him a hug, and Sunny knew from Landry's expression that the spontaneous show of affection was unexpected. He never said much about his childhood, so she had to wonder what it had been like. She knew his parents didn't spend much time in this country.

What did that mean? Her fertile imagination could dredge up all kinds of scenarios ranging from them being on the FBI's Ten Most Wanted list to them conducting a money- laundering scheme.

Sunny's musings about Landry's family took a back seat when she spied Walter with a voluptuous brunette on his arm.

"Are you watching Walter?" Landry whispered, causing goose bumps to scamper up her spine.

"Uh-huh," she murmured. "Look at him. Not a care in the world. How could he commit a murder and then act like…that?" She waved a hand in the air. "And how could I have married him?"

Landry pulled her toward a bench at the edge of the garden. "Let's sit down," he urged. "We need to talk. You need to remember he's only a suspect. At the moment, everything is alleged." Landry was tempted to tell her about Bubba Gene, but decided to speak to the sheriff first.

"Spoken like a true lawyer. Alleged, my rear— you know he did it. I know he did it, and he sure knows he did it," Sunny proclaimed with a pout. "The only thing I can't figure out is why. Was it an accident or did he intend to kill her? I hope to God it was an accident."

That did it. He had to tell her what was happening, but he wanted some privacy to do it. "Are you about ready to go home?"

"Sure," she agreed. However, before they made it to the door, they ran into Lily and Clay.

"Hey, guys, when we find Liza and Charlie we're heading to the pub for a beer. I've had all the canapés I can stand. Want to join us?" Lily asked.

Actually that didn't sound half-bad. The company would be fun, and a cold beer was enticing. Plus it gave Landry a good excuse to procrastinate.

"What do you think?" Sunny looked to him for confirmation.

"I'm game. Let's thank our hostess and beat feet."

Sunny grinned.

"I'm right behind you," she assured him, pushing Landry toward the group of middle-aged women who were hostesses for the shindig.

Chapter 31

"Sunny, it's Uncle Dave. I'd like you and Landry to come down to the office." It was Sunday and Dave didn't normally work on weekends, so she knew it was important.

"Is this about the DNA?"

"Uh-huh. You guys need to come on down."

"Is it good or bad?"

"Thirty minutes?" He was doing the strong silent cop thing.

"We'll be there shortly." She disconnected and punched in Landry's cell number. He was out doing God only knew what. Although their evening had been wonderful, he was acting strange today. "Uncle Dave called and wants us to come to the station. It's about the DNA," she told him when he answered.

"I'll pick you up in a few minutes."

The courthouse wasn't more than five minutes by car from Sunny's house, ten if you encountered a funeral procession. This time the trip seemed interminable.

"I'm nervous," Sunny said, twisting her fingers. "What if I've been accusing Walter of something horrible and he's innocent?" she wailed. "That would make me feel like dog poop. And if he really did it, that's even worse."

"Sunny." Landry pulled over to the side of the road. "I have to tell you something." He turned in the seat to look at her. "I've been trying to figure out how to say this, but I'm a coward. Two days ago I talked to Bubba Gene. He told me that Walter was at Aunt

Hallie's the day of the murder, and that she was alive when he left."

"What?"

"Walter didn't kill Hallie. I'm sure the DNA will prove it." He picked up her hand. "We'll get through this, I promise."

Uncle Dave offered coffee but Sunny was too upset to put a thing in her stomach. Her mouth was so dry she couldn't say a word if her life depended on it.

Landry apparently wasn't working under the same limitation. "Sheriff, sir. I have some new information." He then told Dave about his conversation with Bubba Gene.

"I questioned him and he didn't tell me any of that," Dave said with a rueful expression.

"I guess I lucked into asking him the right question. So I'm assuming the DNA didn't match?"

"Yep." Dave paced from the window to his desk. "Hell of a mess isn't it? Now we're back to square one. I don't believe Bubba Gene did anything and I think the District Attorney is on the same page. I can't tell you any specifics, but we're developing some new ideas."

Later in the evening Sunny and Landry were snuggled on the couch while Miss Priss claimed her favorite spot—his lap. Somehow along the way, Sunny's cat had decided Landry was one of her favorite humans.

"What are we going to do now?"

Landry hesitated before speaking. "*We're* not going to do anything. It's time to leave it to the police."

Sunny sat up and gave Landry one of those

looks. "Even though Walter didn't kill Aunt Hallie, I believe he's the one who has been threatening me, and I intend to prove it. If I don't, I'll never feel safe again."

"We have to trust in the system."

Sunny snorted. "Do you seriously believe justice will be served? An innocent old lady was killed, someone not only shot at us they also tried to torch my business, and the police don't have a shred of evidence. Do you honestly think we can rely on the system?"

Landry was an attorney— he had to believe in the law.

Unfortunately, he was afraid he was about to lose this argument, and that was before Liza called and then Sunny smirked.

Her attitude didn't bode well for Landry's case. "I'll bite. What did she say?" he asked, even though he didn't want to hear the answer.

"Liza said that Charlie had dinner with his developer friend from Austin and guess what the guy said."

Landry was no dummy. He knew when to throw in the towel.

"Beats me."

"According to him, Walter assured them that he's taking care of the problem. I'll bet the farm that the *problem* would be me. It makes sense. Deep down, he's always been angry that I was willing to stand up to his mother and he wasn't. And now he sees me as a threat to his land deal."

Landry couldn't argue with that line of reasoning. "So what do you have in mind?"

Sunny knew the minute she'd won. "Let's

assume we have two separate crimes, the murder and the threats. And let's further presume that Walter is the person who has been terrorizing me. I think we should go at this from a business angle. Let's scare the truth out of him."

"How do you intend to do that?"

"We'll have Charlie talk to his friend. That development company would not be pleased with the bad publicity I'm willing to stir up."

Landry sighed. "If you accuse Walter of something without proof, he can sue you and win."

"I don't plan for it to get that far. My ex is *not* a brave man. He hasn't stood up to Beatrice the Beast in his entire life. We'll let the big guy in Austin do our dirty work for us. All it will take is a few well-placed words and good old Walter will fold like a cheap lawn chair."

Chapter 32

Two days later, Sunny and Raylene were getting ready for the Double Date grand re-Opening when the bell on the front door welcomed a visitor.

"We're in the back," Sunny yelled, expecting to see Landry with a box of Krispy Kremes. Instead, she looked up and saw Walter. Yikes!

"Raylene," Sunny didn't know what else to say.

"I see him, and I have my cell ready to call 911," Raylene muttered.

"Walter, what do you want?"

"I want to talk to you. In private."

Raylene moved toward Sunny in a show of support.

"Raylene stays. You have five minutes to say what you have to say. Then I want you out of here."

Obviously distraught, Walter ran his fingers through his thinning hair. The poor old boy was feeling guilty, and wasn't that too bad. He'd made his bed and now he was in for a prickly lie down.

"Sunny, I, uh, I…"

"Five minutes." She held up five fingers. "Your time is running so you'd better hurry."

"I'm sorry."

"I beg your pardon?"

"I'm really sorry." He hung his head. "I didn't intend to hurt you, honestly I didn't. I started the fire and shot at you, but I just wanted to scare you enough for you to butt out. This real estate deal is my one chance to get away from Port Serenity."

Sunny really, really wanted to beat the stuffing

out of the jerk, but somehow she managed to maintain some semblance of civility. "So you're admitting to the arson, the shooting, the threatening notes *and* the vandalism?"

"Yeah," he mumbled, as he pushed his hands into his pockets. "If I pay for your cleanup and buy you a bunch of new stuff, would you consider getting me off the hook with the Austin boys?"

He looked so contrite; Sunny was tempted to help him, but not quite yet. Regardless of his show of remorse, he'd committed a number of felonies. His career was probably the least of his problems. Uncle Dave was not going to be amused.

"So why did you focus on me instead of Liza or Lily?" That question had bothered her from the very beginning.

"Because I know you better."

"You know me. You bet your sweet rear you know me. We were married!" Sunny could barely contain the screech that was itching to escape. "Here's the deal. I'll get you out of this mess, at least with your business partners, on two conditions. You never talk to me or bother me again. If you see me walking down the street, you'd better hightail it to other side. In fact, I think you'd be happier if you relocated to Austin. And second, you have to confess to Uncle Dave."

"I have to tell the sheriff?" he whined.

"Yes. They say that confession is good for the soul." Sunny put her hands on her hips. That condition was non-negotiable. Dave would make sure Walter faced up to his responsibilities.

He was obviously trying to decide whether he

could live with her ultimatum, but then he capitulated.

"Okay. I'll go see him right now."

"That's a good decision."

"You go, girl," Raylene exclaimed as Walter trudged out the door. "Give me five," she said, raising, her hand in celebration.

"I have some really good news." Sunny had waited until after dinner, dessert, and some good old-fashioned lovin' before she broke the news.

"What?" he asked, kissing her neck and generally distracting them both.

"I talked to Walter today."

Landry sat up so fast he almost dumped her off the bed. "You did what?"

"Walter came by the shop and confessed to pulling all the stunts against me," Sunny said with a smirk. It wasn't very ladylike but she couldn't help herself.

"He confessed?"

"Yep, and he's gonna talk to Uncle Dave."

"I'll be damned. He said he'd leave you alone?"

"Yeah." Sunny told him all about the conversation.

"That's great news," he said, stacking his arms behind his head. "Now let's talk about us." Sunny didn't seem very enthusiastic about this conversation, so Landry decided to put her at ease. And that, of course, required some kisses—one of his favorite pastimes.

He had some life-changing plans in mind. He'd been weighing alternatives for some time. Although it was looking more and more like the charges against

Bubba Gene would be dropped due to lack of evidence, it was obvious the town could use a good defense attorney. Add that professional opportunity to the miracles of modern travel and technology, and Landry felt like he could work part-time with the New Orleans office, while spending most of the year in Port Serenity.

Heck, Wharton and Valliere could even open a Houston office.

"I love you." Landry almost asked her to marry him, but hesitated. This was the one-and-only time he ever intended to ask for anyone's hand, so he wanted to do it right. And that meant a ring in his pocket and a viable relocation plan in place.

"I love you, too," she answered, snuggling closer.

He tweaked her nose and followed up with an erotic nibble on her ear. "Colby called and said there's a glitch with one of my cases," he said. "So I have to go back to New Orleans tomorrow. With Walter out of the picture, I feel a whole lot better leaving you alone." Then he did some more delightful things to her neck, collarbone and areas farther south. "I'll probably be gone at least a week." Talking and kissing was taxing even to Landry's vaunted ability to multitask.

"I want you to come to the Big Easy to meet my friends."

"I can do that." After she started unbuttoning his shirt he wasn't sure what she had agreed to do.

It was true; there was a problem with one of his cases. However, the bigger reason for the trip was to make plans for his future. Two days into his negotiation

193

with Colby, Landry realized the operation would take much longer than he expected. They weren't exactly disassembling their law firm; however, they were undertaking a major reorganization. Fortunately, they weren't in the middle of any high-profile cases so the primary players had the time to concentrate on the new hierarchy.

"Are you sure you want to do this?" Colby asked. They were at the Hair of the Hound enjoying a beer.

"I'm absolutely positive," Landry declared, shooting his partner a grin. "I'm in love."

"Man!" Colby shook his head. "And to think I'm responsible. I guess that means I have to be your best man." He clapped Landry on the back. "I never thought I'd see the day."

"Neither did I," Landry admitted. "You should try it."

Colby pushed his stool back. "Not me, buddy. By the way, when is your fiancée coming up?"

Landry studied his beer before replying. "Actually, I haven't officially asked her to marry me. I'm waiting for the right moment."

Colby glared at his friend. "Let me get this straight. You're turning your professional life upside down, and you haven't asked her?"

"When you put it that way, it sounds pretty stupid, doesn't it."

"Yeah. Dumber than dirt."

Landry knew Colby was right and that made him really nervous. The predicted week had stretched to almost three. He talked to her almost every day, but it wasn't the same. He was antsy to get back to Texas.

"I suggest you get a ring on that girl's finger," Colby said with a frown. "For a smart guy, you have mush for brains.

Chapter 33

"Have you heard from that handsome honey of yours?" Although Joynelle Tucker asked the question, everyone in the salon stopped to listen.

"Sure, I've talked to him. In fact, I'm going to New Orleans for the weekend. He's having a party and wants me to meet his friends," Sunny replied. Since she didn't know exactly where their relationship was going, she wasn't tempted to elaborate. He'd said he loved her, but they hadn't discussed anything permanent.

"That's right nice. Did you get you a new dress?" Viola Horatio asked, but before Sunny could answer, she continued her questions. "Have you heard anything new about the murder?"

Sunny was about to respond when Laverne Hightower rendered everyone speechless. "I've been cogitating about this, and I don't know why I didn't think of it before. Did you know that Crumpy and Hallie Rule were sweethearts back before the war?"

"The war?" Sunny asked.

"World War II."

"Crumpy and Aunt Hallie dated?" Sunny hated to sound obtuse, but that didn't make any sense.

"Yep. Don't know why those two never got hitched. I suspect it had something to do with their families. That and the fact they fought all the time. Age didn't improve their dispositions, none at all," Laverne cackled in glee. "It was all a big secret. Only Hallie's very best friends knew. Even her family was kept in the dark. If you want my opinion, Crumpy's your guy."

Good grief! How had *that* bit of information

escaped the attention of the rumor-mongers? And had Uncle Dave discovered *any* of it during his investigation.

"We have to talk, so why don't you guys meet me at the Dew Drop Inn," Sunny said without preamble.

"Yes, ma'am," Liza agreed with a chuckle. "Any particular time your majesty would like us to appear?" she asked.

"Can it, cuz, and let's make it five o'clock."

"Now you have my curiosity up. We'll be there."

The Dew Drop Inn wasn't their normal stomping ground, but the tavern seemed like the perfect place to discuss murder and mayhem.

"I ordered margaritas and nachos," Sunny informed her cousins when they arrived.

"Merciful heavens, I hope this discussion doesn't require tequila," Lily said, dropping her purse into an empty chair.

"Me, too," Liza agreed with a frown.

Sunny waited until the waitress delivered their drinks before she proceeded. "Here's the deal. I want to go out to Crumpy Hardaway's place to do some investigating."

"No way! You *are* nuts," Lily exclaimed.

Considering Lily was always ready for an adventure, that wasn't a good sign, but Sunny forged ahead.

"You'll never guess what Laverne Hightower told us." After Sunny finished her story, it took several minutes for the cousins to process the new information.

"So, what do you want us to do?" Liza asked.

"And why aren't you going to Uncle Dave with this?" Lily chimed in.

"I made such a huge deal about Walter that I don't think Uncle Dave will believe me. Not unless I have something more to go on than Laverne Hightower's word. You remember that he and Laverne aren't exactly buddies."

"That's the truth! She'd just as soon gut him with an oyster knife as look at him," Lily said. "So what do you want us to do?"

"Let's go out there right now."

"Right now?" Liza squeaked.

"Yes, right now. It's five o'clock and his worthless grandsons will be at the bar."

"There is that," Lily agreed. "Let's do it." She picked up her purse, ready for action.

"Are we absolutely sure this is a good idea?" Liza asked, as their car fell into a pothole the size of an eight-person hot tub.

Even Sunny was having doubts about the wisdom of this little jaunt. "Look out," she yelled, as Lily drove them straight into another abyss.

"I think we've found the right address." Liza indicated a clearing where several rusted trailers sat amid a sea of derelict cars and ancient appliances.

"I've seen junk farms, but this one takes the cake." Lily hit the automatic locks. "Unless St. Peter comes out of that place with an engraved invitation, we're not getting out of this car."

"Ye gods, that dog looks rabid," Liza screamed. The canine in question had jumped up and was going nose-to-nose with Sunny through the window.

"Yikes!" Sunny jerked away, almost strangling herself on the seat belt.

"This wasn't such a good idea, huh?" Sunny hated to admit it, but this appeared to be another in a long line of mistakes.

"Look, there's Crumpy." Lily indicated a wizened old man who was stalking across the beaten-down grass.

"That man fell out of the ugly tree and hit every branch on the way down." The pithy remark came from Liza.

Life hadn't been kind to Crumpy Hardaway.

"What do you gals want?" he demanded, thumping on the window.

"Do we roll it down?" Sunny asked.

"No!"

"Yes," Lily said, countermanding her sister.

Sunny compromised by cracking open the window. "We want to talk to you about Hallie Rule's death."

Apparently she'd uttered the magic words. With a huff, a puff and a grimace, he conceded. "Come on in, if ya have to. Makes no never mind to me," he said and then marched toward the trailer. The dog gave a whimper and followed him.

"Are you really going in there" Liza asked, looking a smidge green.

Sunny hesitated. This was her big idea, but was she willing to risk dying? That was highly unlikely, though, wasn't it? "If we want to get to the truth, we have to gut up and talk to him. Right?"

Lily nodded reluctantly.

"There are three of us and one of him. What can he do?" Liza said, although she didn't say it with much conviction.

"Let's go." Sunny hopped out of the car. She hoped her cousins would follow, and she wasn't disappointed.

Lily marched around the front of the car and linked arms with Sunny and Liza. "There's safety in numbers. Let's do it."

Together the three marched into the lion's den— aka Crumpy's trailer.

"Sit yourselves down if you want. I'll tell you right off I don't have nothing to say." He was ensconced in a massive recliner with the dog at his feet.

Sunny sat gingerly on an ancient couch that was repaired with duct tape. Liza was apparently trying to find something wooden to sit on, but failing that she joined her cousin. Lily plopped down beside them.

"I already talked to the sheriff. Told him he'd better leave my family alone or I'd have his badge. "Crumpy slapped his knee. "That's a good one. Knew his father, ya know. That old man was as stubborn as his kid. Dave's a purty good sheriff, but that's neither here nor there. All my family's got alibis for each other. He ain't got nothing on us."

Sunny had to wonder what the "nothing" was. Did that mean Crumpy was responsible for Aunt Hallie's death? Or was he covering for one of his relatives? What would Nancy Drew do?

Nancy would go straight for the jugular. "I understand you were in love with Hallie. Why didn't you get married?"

He appeared shocked, but recovered quickly. "Where'd you hear that, girlie?" He didn't quite shout, but it was apparent the question bothered him.

"Everyone at the beauty salon knows." Thanks to Laverne Hightower.

Crumpy closed his eyes as if to go back in time. "I loved that girl. She was the purtiest thing I ever seen. We started sneakin' around way back before the war, and then I was drafted." He rubbed his forehead. "When I got back she was married. Her old man knew we were sweet on each other, so he made sure she was off the market. I never got over her. You don't forget the first person you love." He seemed deep in thought.

Sunny felt bad for him, and her cousins seemed equally sympathetic. "So, do you know anything that could help us find the person who hurt her?"

The old man shook his head. He had tears in his eyes. "Might as well tell you, my conscience is makin' me twitchy. My boys don't understand. They say just keep my mouth shut and it'll go away, but I don't want the memory of Hallie to go away. I didn't mean to hurt her."

Sunny's mouth dropped open. He was going to confess.

Crumpy's story was a strange mixture of *Romeo and Juliet* and *Bonnie and Clyde*. Their love affair had been thwarted, but as neighbors they'd maintained a distant, but amicable relationship. Until the specter of big money popped up. Then everything went to hell in a handbasket.

201

"I went over there to talk to her. All I wanted was a nice, civilized powwow. Damnation, she had more money than she could ever use and we're poor as church mice. The way I figured, we could split the money evenly. But no way. She wanted it all."

He paused to gather his thoughts. "She started screaming at me. Then she tried to hit me with a fireplace poker. I shoved her and that's when it happened. She wasn't none too sure on her feet so she fell and hit her head. I checked her pulse and there wasn't none. Damn, those head wounds bleed a lot." By that time, tears were flowing down his weathered cheeks. "I never meant to hurt her, I loved her."

It was an unfortunate accident, not a murder. Wasn't *that* something?

Sunny was on her cell calling Uncle Dave before Crumpy's dog stopped chasing their car. The cousins were back at the Dew Drop Inn having a debriefing session over a plate of nachos and a pitcher of margaritas.

"Can you believe he confessed?" Liza shook her head in disbelief. "Normal people don't do things like that."

"Crumpy's not normal," Lily asserted, pouring another round of drinks. "What charges do you think he'll face?

"I don't know." Sunny shrugged. "All I know is that I'm thrilled the charges against Bubba Gene are going to be dropped. I feel sorry for Crumpy. He really did love Aunt Hallie and it was an accident."

Liza and Lily nodded their agreement.

"Do you think we'll have to find Crumpy a lawyer?" Lily asked.

"Maybe I can talk Landry into representing him." Sunny's giggle was a combination of tequila overload and a vision of cool, sophisticated Landry taking on the king of rednecks.

"Speaking of your handsome boyfriend," Lily said, crunching on another chip. "Tell me exactly what he said about this shindig you're going to."

"He didn't tell me squat, other than he was giving a party and I should dress up."

"Hmm," Liza murmured.

"So, what are his intentions?" That question came from Lily. The girl was nosy beyond belief. "Are you going to marry him and move to, uh...New Orleans?"

"None of you business!"

Ignoring Sunny, Lily continued the questioning. "So is a wedding in the future?"

"We haven't discussed marriage, so I think it's a bit premature to select bridesmaid's dresses. And that's the last I'm going to say on the matter. For now, anyway," Sunny said with a giggle.

Chapter 34

The day before she left for New Orleans was a whirlwind of activity. Sunny was in the salon's storeroom checking the inventory of shampoo when her cell phone rang. Was it in her pocket? Of course not.

Was it on the front counter? More than likely.

That would have been okay if she hadn't tripped over a box and landed on her derriere. So once again, Landry's voice found its way to her voicemail.

"Hi, sweetheart. Just calling to see what you're doing and to find out what time your flight gets in." There was a pause and she could hear conversation in the background. "I've gotta go. Talk to you later. Love ya."

His voice was a perfect combination of a velvety baritone with just a little New Orleans accent mixed in. No wonder he could mesmerize a jury.

No sooner did she hit the disconnect button when the cell chirped again. This time it was Lily.

"What time do we need to leave for the airport?"

"Early, really early. How about six o'clock?"

"Great, I love predawn travel." That was the biggest lie in the world. Lily was *not* a morning person. "Have you talked to that handsome man of yours lately?"

"Not for a day or two," Sunny replied with a sigh. "I just got another voice mail."

She missed him like crazy. In fact, Sunny couldn't wait to get to get her hands on him. For sure, there was gonna be some kissin', cuddling, and other good stuff in her very near future.

The alarm clock jarred her out of a deep sleep. Darn, she was in the middle of some hot, wild sex.

"Sheesh," Sunny muttered, hitting the snooze button. She was about to dive under her pillow when she got a whiff of fresh brewed coffee. It was the elixir of the gods, cure of all ills—wonderful caffeine-laden java, guaranteed to give her a kick start. Thank God for automatic coffee pots.

Sunny had just finished zipping her bag when Lily barged in the kitchen.

"I'd kill for a cup of coffee," she said, rummaging through the cupboard for a cup.

Sunny would have laughed at the sight of her cousin's desperation. However, she'd felt the same way.

"Let's get rolling. We have at least an hour's drive and that doesn't account for traffic or something weird happening on the bridge." Lily grabbed the suitcase and headed to the car. "It wouldn't surprise me to find a traffic jam."

Unfortunately, those words proved to be prophetic.

Their undoing, however, was a jackknifed semi on the freeway.

"Do you think all these people get up at this ungodly time every morning?" Lily complained," Lily complained, looking over the sea of cars and trucks going to the chemical plants and the Corpus Christi port.

"The next exit we creep up to, I'm getting off this highway. You'll miss your flight if we don't get movin'," she declared, taking stock of the situation. "In fact, I'm going to drive up the shoulder to that next exit.

Watch for cops," Lily instructed, seconds before she pulled onto the shoulder.

"This is so illegal it hurts." Sunny held onto the armrest and prayed they wouldn't get arrested or even worse, killed. "It's a good thing you have a 4x4. That concrete median you ran over would have wrecked anything else."

Lily responded with a grin. "Hang on, you're not gonna be late."

Miraculously, they made it to the airport with a few minutes to spare. After a delay at security, Sunny made it to her gate in the nick of time.

"You'd better run for it, honey, they're about to close the door," the ticket taker yelled as she charged down the jet way.

She dashed into the first class cabin seconds before the flight attendant slammed the door closed. Traveling was incredibly stressful.

Sunny was battling a bad case of nerves as she made her way through the crowd at the New Orleans airport. What was wrong with her? She loved Landry and he loved her. Didn't he?

The good news was her luggage made it. The bad news was Landry was a no-show.

"Miss McAllister, over here."

Sunny scanned the crowd for the owner of the voice. Much to her dismay, it came from a gaunt man with a large a red and purple dragon tattoo on his bicep. He was holding a sign with her name on it.

She hesitated a moment, then took the plunge. "I'm Sunny McAllister. Did Mr. Valliere send you?"

"Yes, ma'am, I'm at your service. You can call me Tommy. Do you have everything?"

Sunny nodded, unable to come up with an articulate comment.

"Let me carry your things." He didn't wait for her to answer before grabbing her bag and heading to the exit. It was hard to reconcile the man's rough exterior with his amazingly elegant manners.

"I was expecting Landry. Do you know why he asked you to pick me up?"

"No, ma'am, I surely don't. He told me to tell you that he had a crisis at work and he'd see you at the house."

"Do you have a key so I can get in?" Sunny thought about asking him drop her at a hotel.

"No, ma'am, you won't need a key. Darlene's at home. Right about now, the place will be crawling with caterers and cleaners for the party tonight."

Now she really was confused. Caterers and cleaners? What happened to the little get-together she expected?

"Who is Darlene?"

"She's Mr. Valliere's housekeeper, and even better she's my wife. Everyone's been running around like chickens with their heads cut off trying to pull this party together." Tommy smiled as if he had a big secret.

Okay, she owned a designer dress and through some miracle it had made it through the hell of airline travel; however, that was irrelevant to the misgivings Sunny was having about this party. Caterers, housekeepers—what next—a string quartet and the prince of Lichtenstein?

"Wait right here, little lady, and I'll bring the car around," Tommy instructed as he deposited her luggage on the sidewalk. "I'll be right back."

"Don't bother. I'll come with you."

"Can't do that, it wouldn't be proper. Besides this is my job. Why don't you wait with the luggage? I'll be right back."

It was his job? Good grief! He was a chauffeur. What *had* she gotten herself into?

Sunny was so caught up in her thoughts she didn't notice the sleek black Mercedes slide to a stop in front of her.

"Miss McAllister, why don't you get on in the car while I put your things in the trunk?" Tommy popped the trunk with the remote and opened the back door for her.

Landry had a Mercedes and a driver? Now her curiosity was on overload. Sunny knew he was a partner in a law firm; so she'd assumed he was doing okay. However, that was a world away from being filthy rich. The way things were looking, she suspected his bank balance was in the millions.

Why would he want a small-town girl with a Wal-Mart wardrobe—especially one with such a humble beginning?

"Is Mr. Valliere your employer?"

"He sure is," Tommy announced proudly.

"Are you his driver?" Call her curious—or more likely, just plain old nosy.

"I'm more of a handy-man. I do whatever needs to be done around the house. I drive and do whatever."

The more questions Sunny asked, the more

uncomfortable Tommy looked. Not that she could blame him, she sounded like a prosecutor.

"He's incredibly wealthy, isn't he?"

Tommy didn't have to say a thing; his flushed cheeks were answer enough.

"I'm sorry." Sunny didn't want to make it awkward for him. After all, he wasn't the person who had skipped over some very important details—like being as wealthy as Croesus. "Do I have any other surprises to look forward to?"

"Well, ma'am, I guess that depends on how easy you are to surprise. I suspect you have some more coming." He paused before continuing. "If you want a piece of advice from a country boy, I think you should just take things as they come, and enjoy the ride. Everything will be fine, just fine. Take old Tommy's word for it. Darlene will love pampering you."

Before Sunny could process that information, he changed the subject. "Have you been to New Orleans before?"

She sat back and vaguely listened to Tommy's travelogue. The longer Sunny tried to put the puzzle pieces together; the more certain she was they wouldn't ever fit.

He was a wealthy attorney—she owned a beauty salon.

He was a sophisticated city dweller—she loved living in a small town.

Damn, he probably ate duck pate—and her favorite food was pimento cheese.

Holy tamoley! If she kept thinking this way, her head would blow up like the folks in the *Kingsman* movie. Unfortunately, she didn't know the half of it. When Tommy stopped the car in the front of an elegant New Orleans' antebellum mansion, she almost busted a button.

"We're here. Sit right where you are, little lady. I'll have you inside in just a minute." The speed with which Tommy jumped out of the vehicle indicated he was afraid she'd make a run for it. Smart man.

He quickly opened the door and helped her out to the sidewalk. "Let me take you in and introduce you to Darlene. Then I'll come back and get your stuff," he said, guiding her up the stairs to a wrap-around porch and a ten-panel door topped by a cut glass fanlight.

This was turning into a Cinderella moment. Sunny had grown up in a beautiful house, but Landry's home was…what could you say other than it was palatial. And that was merely a description of the exterior. With its elegant marble foyer, spiral staircase and massive crystal chandelier, the interior was even more impressive.

Yep, Sunny had suddenly morphed into the country cousin.

"Jeeze, Louise. That thing's got to be Waterford," she muttered under her breath.

A faint chuckle told her she'd committed the ultimate social faux pas. Commenting on brands was almost as gauche as flipping over a dinner plate to check the label. She turned to find Tommy with his arm around a short, chubby woman. Sunny finally managed to dredge up some semblance of dignity and extended her hand. "You must be Darlene. I'm Sunny McAllister."

Instead of shaking Sunny's hand, Darlene enveloped her in a hug.

"Well, if you aren't just as cute as a button."

Was Darlene going to pinch her cheek?

"Adorable. Tommy, isn't she darling?"

What could you say to that, other than thank you?

"Come with me and I'll show you your room," Darlene cooed. "You can get all settled. Then I'll bring you a snack. Mr. Landry called and asked me to tell you he had some things to do at the office, but he'd be home as soon as possible."

"Oh, okay," Sunny said, following the housekeeper up the stairs.

"Mr. Landry told me to put you in here, but if you'd prefer someplace else, I can do that, too." Darlene opened the door to an elegant suite of rooms decorated in masculine shades of navy and burgundy. The décor screamed testosterone.

"No, this'll be fine." But would it really be? Sunny was having a major lapse of confidence. This was Landry's environment, and she'd never in a million years fit.

"Just make yourself at home." Darlene said as she and Tommy turned to leave.

That wasn't going to be easy. The house reeked of old money and New World aristocracy. Regardless of the fact that she'd had a wonderful childhood, Sunny had started life at the Willow Brook Mobile Home Park.

When in doubt, she called in the troops, and of course, that meant ringing up one of the cousins.

"We need to talk." Sunny didn't bother with a

211

salutation when Liza answered.

"What's wrong?"

"Landry has this mansion with a housekeeper, and a driver, and probably a full team of gardeners."

"What do you mean by a mansion?"

"I mean a frickin' mansion that has a Waterford chandelier the size of a Honda."

"In the Garden District?"

"Like duh."

"Do you know how much real estate goes for in that area?" Leave it to Liza, the uber developer, to have the information at her fingertips.

"Mega-millions, I imagine."

"Absolutely. So, you're telling me he's rich and you're feeling out of your element."

"What should I do?" Sunny couldn't contain the wail that had been itching to break out ever since she laid eyes on the Valliere digs.

There was a pause. "You're going to put your chin up and remember everything that Anna Belle and Eugenie taught you. You're a lady right down to the tips of your toes. You know how to use a fish fork."

Liza was right, by golly, she was correct. "Okay, I get it. I can do this." Sunny's confidence was somewhat undermined by the sniffle that managed to sneak by her defenses. "He worked as my shampoo guy. How embarrassing is that?"

"It was his choice."

True. "But what do I do about him being filthy rich?"

"Enjoy it? He loves you."

"Yeah, yeah, okay. I vaguely remember him

telling me he has a trust fund. So I suppose he wasn't trying to keep anything from me. That should make me feel better, right?"

"That's a girl. Chin up. Remember, fish fork."

"Gotcha." A talk with one of her cousins always put a smile on her face.

Feeling much better, Sunny was preparing to unpack when Darlene tapped on the door.

"I brought you some tea and sandwiches. And here's a cold bottle of wine. This should keep hunger at bay until the party. I told that boy I could do all the cooking, but he insisted on getting a caterer," Darlene kept up a running monologue. "He said it would be too much trouble. Mr. Landry is such a considerate man. You know I've worked for his family since he was little."

This seemed like the perfect opportunity to get some information about Landry's folks.

"I didn't know that. What are they like?"

Darlene looked as if she was trying to decide how much to say, then she sighed. "They have a house in the south of France. Ever since Mr. Valliere retired that's where they spend most of their time.

They have a house in the south of France. Wow!

"Mr. Valliere's a nice man. I think that's why Landry is such a thoughtful guy." The housekeeper paused. "And as far as Mrs. Valliere goes, let's just say she's...something else." Darlene snapped her mouth shut.

Was that a euphemism for a snob or a witch?

The housekeeper bustled around the room straightening items that didn't need straightening.

"She's always trying to fix Mr. Landry up with one of those snotty social girls. Swear to goodness, if that woman isn't meddling, she isn't happy. Miss Kristen usually ignores her mom. I say good for her. "Now what else can I do for you?

The font of information had apparently dried up.

"I don't need anything else, thank you."

"All right," Darlene said, putting her hands on her ample hips. "Let me know if you need me, ya hear."

"Yes, ma'am."

Sunny's response prompted a chuckle from the housekeeper. "You're as adorable as a speckled pup."

That time Sunny wasn't spared the cheek pinch.

"Why don't you go find that bathtub and take a long soak? I left some nice bubble bath for you. Swear to goodness, you could put half the Saints football team in that thing."

A bottle of wine and a hot soak sounded like heaven. Welcome to the life of the Rich and Famous.

What to do next—paint her toenails, kick back with some wine, catch a cab back to the airport? Not surprisingly, the wine option won.

The stiffly elegant décor was undoubtedly the work of a very high priced interior decorator. It was beautiful, but it didn't reflect the man she knew intimately. In fact, the house looked like it came out of *Architectural Digest*. It didn't have that lived-in look. There wasn't a litter box in sight. Miss Priss would hate it.

Landry had seemed so comfortable in her home. He never denied her spoiled calico a lap when she made one of her arrogant demands. How could someone who

214

lived in all this opulence seem so down home? And that brought her to the real question. Did she *really* know him?

Chapter 35

"You must be Miss McAllister."

Sunny was jerked out of her musings by a gorgeous brunette who glided through the open door as if she owned the world. And from the looks of her outfit, she probably did—own the world, that is

"I'm Amelie Barrois." She picked up the wine bottle and checked the label. "It looks like Darlene did it again," she sighed. Even her disparaging remark was done with a sexy French accent. "She makes a lot of mistakes, but Landry darling is so terribly fond of her, he keeps her on. I always thought he should get European help. They have a much better concept of protocol and etiquette. Don't you agree?" She gave Sunny the same look of disapproval she had previously reserved for the domestic brand of chardonnay.

"Landry and I have been inseparable for..." she gave an eloquent Gallic shrug "...forever. Our parents are old friends. I'll never forget that summer he spent at our villa in Provence. I frequently serve as his hostess. Did you know that?" Her smile hinted at something far more intimate than hostess duties.

Sunny couldn't believe what she was hearing. Landry had told her about Amelie, but the way he talked about her, she was gone from his life. This stunning woman certainly didn't act like she was in the past tense.

"I'm terribly embarrassed Darlene put you in this room. But to give her the benefit of the doubt, maybe Landry didn't tell her." Amelie leaned forward as if indicating she was about to impart a secret.

"Tell me what?" A feeling of dread was seeping

through Sunny's pores. The last time she'd felt like this was the day Mama didn't come home. This was not looking good.

"Well, it's something of a secret, but last night Landry and I came to an understanding." The debutante elegantly crossed her legs and continued. "I feel certain we'll be announcing our engagement within the month. It takes a considerable amount of time to prepare a wedding appropriate for our families."

Sunny appreciated how a mongoose might feel. Despite the Armani outfit, this woman was nothing but a snake.

"I know you think you got rather close to my Landry. But frankly, he's like that. He didn't have the heart to tell you about us on the phone, so I decided to spare him the embarrassment. Besides, he felt he owed you a nice trip."

Amelie rose and wandered toward the bed. "Naturally, I'll have Darlene move your things to the guest room." She turned to face Sunny, "I hope this hasn't been too inconvenient, but I'm sure you understand."

To say Sunny had a belly full of this bitch was an understatement of massive proportions. And apparently she wasn't finished talking.

"Please take as long as you want to pack. Darlene will take care of your suitcases. I'll be downstairs going over the last-minute preparations with the caterer." With that zinger she exited.

What chutzpah. Was this a case of ultimate BS or merely the truth? Damn! Why *hadn't* Landry meet her at the airport?

217

Emergency—her rear end!

When you got down to the heart of the matter, they hadn't talked in a couple of days. And when he did leave a message he sounded distracted. It was conceivable that something had happened in that length of time—including reconciling with Miss Cotillion.

However, and this was a big however, perhaps Darlene wasn't privy to the "dump Sunny" plan. Maybe Landry wanted a little farewell party before he and what's-her-name announced their joyful union.

Would anyone in their right mind make up something that outrageous? Highly unlikely—unless they were delusional, and Miss Rich Bitch looked like she was in complete control of her faculties

Outrage. Embarrassment. A dollop of insecurity.

All that was all irrelevant. Obviously he'd slipped back into the sophisticated urban life and left the poor beautician in the dust.

Men—bah, humbug! They couldn't be honest about anything—money, women, jobs anything. She was outta there!

Sunny spied the phone on the bedside table and found the number for the airline. When in doubt, the best thing to do was leave the party.

"I need the first flight you have to Corpus Christi, the quicker the better."

"I have a six forty-five through Houston. Let me see if I can get you on it." Sunny could hear the click of computer keys. "Let's see, hmm, the only ticket I have left is in business class."

"That'll be fine." It didn't matter whether it maxed out her credit card. She had to leave.

The ticket taken care of, Sunny's next chore was to find a taxi. She couldn't ask Tommy for a ride. Time was at a premium, so Sunny tossed her clothes and toiletries back in her bag, scribbled a note and left it where Landry would find it.

She wasn't sneaking out with her tail between her legs. No ma'am. Sunny's good manners forced her to drop her bags and find Darlene to thank her for her hospitality.

"What do you mean you're going home? You can't leave," Darlene exclaimed, wringing her hands.

"Believe me, this is for the best, honestly it is," Sunny said, trying to console the distraught housekeeper. "Amelie told me all about their engagement. There's no way I'm sticking around while they make the happy announcement." She put her arms around her new friend. "It'll be fine. They won't even miss me." Tears were close to the surface, so she didn't dare say much more.

"Oh, no, honey. That's not true." The housekeeper grabbed her arm. "You need to stay until Mr. Landry gets home. He'll iron the whole thing out. I'll bet my bottom dollar this is something Mr. Landry's mother cooked up. She's always wanted him to marry that snob."

"I'm sorry." Sunny heard a car horn. "My cab's here. I have to go. Anytime you get a hankering for a visit to the Texas Gulf Coast, my house is always open."

Darlene grabbed the phone the minute Sunny walked out the door.

Chapter 36

The bad news was the meeting had lasted far longer than Landry anticipated. The good news was it was going well. By the time it ended, the arrangements that would dramatically alter his professional and personal life would be complete.

The woman who'd wormed her way into his heart was about to turn his world on its head—new wife, new home, and a considerable deviation in the course of his professional life.

Sunny, her wacky friends, and her slightly eccentric family would be his when she said yes to his proposal. And that question—and answer—would come as soon as he could get home. He patted his pocket and felt the small ring box. Soon, very soon, he'd have the diamond on her finger.

Landry's interlude in New Orleans had seemed like forever, but now Sunny was here. And much to his delight, Darlene had bestowed her seal of approval.

If the yakking went on much longer he'd have to call it quits. He had plans to make and a pretty lady to kiss.

The party would serve several functions, both personal and professional. On the business side, he wanted to use the opportunity to explain the reconfiguration of the firm. On the fun side, he couldn't wait to introduce Sunny to his friends and colleagues. He had no doubt they'd be charmed and envious. His plans were in place, and now all he had to do was get home to pop the question.

Colby was about to start on the second chorus of

yada, yada, yada when Landry's secretary slipped into the conference room.

"Mr. Valliere," she whispered, "your housekeeper called and said you have to get home right now. Your guest left."

At first he couldn't make any sense of what she was saying. "Who has left?"

"She said Miss McAllister took a cab to the airport."

That got his attention. "Colby, I've got to go, something's happening at home." He didn't wait for an answer before he sprinted out the door.

"Darlene, Darlene," Landry bellowed, running into the house. "What happened? Why did Sunny leave?"

"I think it was that Amelie woman." Darlene underlined her allegation with a snort. "She's here all dressed up and bossing the caterers around. Miss Sunny said Amelie told her you two were getting engaged."

"What?"

"She's still in the dining room if you want to talk to her."

"You bet I do." Amelie Barrios was a pain in the rear. To say she threw herself at him was putting it mildly. It all started when he made the mistake of going to her family home in France. From that point on, she'd assumed they would eventually get married. Then he made the even bigger blunder of dating her. That was when his mother had started shopping for wedding invitations.

Landry stomped down the hall. He was aching for a fight but trying like heck to control his temper.

Getting mad at Amelie tended to send her into hysterics—and that was the last thing he needed. This mess had his mother's fingerprints all over it.

"What have you done this time?" That was reasonably calm.

"Why, hello, darling. I knew you needed some help with your party, so I came over early." Amelie had simpering down to a fine art.

"Why don't you sit down? We need to talk." Hanging on to his composure by a thread, Landry continued. "I want you to know that I'm planning to marry Sunny McAllister." He emphasized the point by pulling the ring case out of his pocket.

"I want you to tell me precisely what you said to her."

Amelie smiled. "I just pointed out that I usually serve as your hostess and I may have hinted we're going to announce our engagement tonight. Your mother told me about the party and everything else."

Yep, his mom was the villain in this piece. "I don't care what my mother thinks. I'm going to say this only once. We are not getting engaged, not now, not ever. You're being delusional if you think otherwise. I want you to leave." His limited patience was almost at an end. "If you're not gone in about three seconds, I'm going to toss your butt out on the street."

Nope, calm and quiet wasn't his forte. That's exactly the reason he hadn't gone into the diplomatic corps. Landry ignored Amelie's declarations of love as he grabbed his phone and stalked out the door.

He spied Darlene lurking in the dining room door. "Please pack me a bag while I call Colby and tell him what's happened. He'll have to play host for me tonight."

Landry was in for some world-class groveling. So bring it on! He was ready.

Sunny felt like a bag lady. Her eyes were red and swollen, her head was about to blow up and she generally felt like crap, with a capital C.

Although it wasn't late when they landed in Corpus Christi, it had been a long and *very* eventful day, and other than renting a car Sunny didn't have any way to get home.

The shuttle didn't run at night, and she wasn't up to dealing with her friends or family. They were so buttinski, they'd either be dripping in sympathy or they'd be ready to organize a necktie party.

Sunny briefly, very briefly, considered hopping the next plane to Timbuktu. That way when she finally got home, she could pretend she and Landry had had a great time but mutually decided to call it quits. Nope. That was the chicken way to handle adversity, and Sunny McAllister was made of sterner stuff. She never clucked her way through a bad situation.

And if you believed that, the Brooklyn Bridge was for sale.

Rejecting a quick get-away to Cancun, she opted for a hotel room and worrying about explaining her early return tomorrow. She *so* did not want to look an idiot!

Aargh! That was Sunny's version of a primal scream; actually, considering security and everything else, it was more of a grunt, but you get the drift. This was *so* not one of her better days.

Snag her luggage. Find a hotel. Get a grip! As far as self-motivation mantras went, that wasn't exactly stellar, but it would have to do.

She followed the crowd to the baggage claim area. What was the carousel number? Jeeze, if she couldn't remember something that simple, her belongings would likely be lost forever in the bowels of the airport.

"Pardon me, pardon me, that one's mine. Would you grab it?" she exclaimed, as her suitcase slid by. Perhaps her luck had changed. Someone down the line hefted it off the belt. Hurray for good Samaritans. However, when Good Sam dropped Sunny's bag at her feet she almost had a coronary.

"What's a nice girl like you doing in a place like this?" Landry didn't wait for her to answer before he continued, "Don't you think we have some things to talk about?"

This was *not* a rational girl's fantasy. She looked like a derelict and he was scrumptious enough to eat with a spoon. Where was the justice in that! And how did he get to Corpus Christi?

"Why aren't you at home?" That was a stupid thing to say. "I mean, what are you doing here?" Great, that was even more obtuse. Escape seemed to be the best option, so Sunny reached for the suitcase. Perhaps she could get outside and grab a cab before he realized what she was up to.

Landry was smarter than that. "To answer your question, I flew in on a chartered plane. And you aren't going anywhere without me." He made a preemptive grab for the handle.

"Give me my bag," Sunny yelped. Uh-oh. People were staring. She grabbed the suitcase with both hands just as he released the handle and reached in his pocket. Yep, you got it—she landed on the floor with a splat.

"Miss, is there a problem?" The airport security guy was not amused. Great! Wouldn't that be the icing on the cake? They could get arrested for brawling in baggage claim.

"I'm sorry, Officer, we were just clowning around. Truly, there's nothing to be concerned about." She gave the man with the gun one of her biggest smiles, and quickly discovered that most of her fellow travelers had abandoned any pretense of disinterest and were blatantly staring.

The way the cop was glaring at Landry she was afraid he was about to read him his Miranda rights. "Are you positive there isn't a problem?" He turned his attention back to Sunny.

"Absolutely, but thank you anyway."

"Okay, if you're sure." Spearing Landry with a final look, the security guard strolled to the escalator.

"Let's get out of here. We can finish this fight someplace private," she hissed.

"That sounds like a plan to me," he replied, grabbing the handle of her bag.

Sunny didn't have much of a choice but to follow, and amazingly he didn't head to a shuttle, or even a taxi. He went straight to a limo at the curb.

"Where are we going?" Sunny squeaked.

"We're going to a hotel."

"No, we're not. Not with me looking like this."
She opened her arms in an all-encompassing gesture.

Landry gave her one of his knee-knocking smiles
and pushed an errant lock of hair behind her ear. "I had a
wonderful plan that included roses and champagne, but
it seems I misplaced the most important player.
Apparently the romance thing isn't going to happen, so
here goes."

He got down on one knee, ignoring the looks
they were getting. The next thing she knew, he was
holding a small black velvet box.

"What's that?" Her voice went up an octave.
Damn it, she hated it when she sounded like Minnie
Mouse. What a dim-witted question. Of course she
recognized a ring box.

Landry flipped open the lid to reveal a diamond
the size of a large marble.

"Sunny McAllister, I want you to be my wife,
for now and always. I love you. Do you love me?"

"Oh, yeah." In the annals of affirmative answers,
that wasn't exactly Shakespeare, but hey, it worked.

"If you hadn't run off you would've found out
that I've made plans to move to Port Serenity."

"Why?" she whispered. How could a slick big-
city lawyer find happiness in a small Texas town?

"Because I love you and we're meant to be
together." He slid his finger down her cheek.

Good answer. Actually, it wasn't merely good, it
was the very best.

"I'm so sorry I messed this up. I should've told
you what I was planning."

She had to agree with that.

So," he said with a grin. "Will you marry me, even if I do have a terrible sense of timing? We can live in your house, or buy a house, or whatever you want."

She stopped his rambling with a resounding yes that was enthusiastic enough to have garnered an audience. That was the last thing she noticed before he sealed their agreement with a long, lazy kiss.

Epilogue

"This is what I call a bridesmaid's dress." Liza did a twirl showing off her cobalt-blue sheath. "I can wear it to a fancy restaurant," she announced. "Not that I ever have a date, but hope springs eternal."

"You look gorgeous and so do I," her twin said. "And the bride is stunning."

Landry and Sunny had decided on a no-frills wedding, so the nuptials were to be held at the gazebo. They felt it was the most appropriate setting.

"Do I look okay?" Sunny asked. "Honest answer." Of course she did. They'd foraged through every retail establishment in Houston. It wasn't exactly haute couture, but it was beautiful. And even better, it was a bargain.

"You couldn't be any prettier," Lily said through her tears. "Group hug."

When the ladies finally disengaged themselves, Liza wiped her eyes. "And don't worry, we won't tell your new mother-in-law, the one who bought her dress in Paris, where we found this number." She fingered the soft blue silk of Sunny's sheath.

"Okay, I guess I'm ready. Make sure I don't have any mascara under my eyes. I don't want to look like a raccoon in our pictures."

"Check, no raccoon eyes. Now let's bustle to the gazebo and get you married."

Uncle Dave chauffeured them in his squad car, lights blazing. Sunny felt like it was appropriate since they'd all been instrumental in solving the mystery of Aunt Hallie. Mama would've been so proud, and she'd *love* Landry.

Oops, tears threatened to reappear. Tears of happiness. Sunny thought about her husband-to-be. He was sexy, fun and the love of her life. The sun was shining, flowers were in bloom, she had fantastic family and friends, and she best of all she was marrying the greatest guy in the world.

All in all, things couldn't get much better.

"Here we are, girls," Dave announced the bridal party's arrival with a blare of the siren.

Aunt Eugenie knocked on his window and when he rolled it down she let him have it. "I've told you over and over not to do that. I thought I was going to have to do CPR on Mrs. Stackhouse. And, if I was forced to blow in that woman's mouth you would have never heard the end of it."

He looked sheepish, but he was still grinning.

"We have a wedding to attend," Liza said, jumping out of the car, pulling Sunny with her.

When Sunny started down the aisle, accompanied by Anna Belle and Joe and Dave and Eugenie, Raylene, Toolie and Penny whooped and hollered to beat the band. Even her soon-to-be father-in-law got into the spirit of things. Who would have ever suspected you could mingle fried shrimp with pâte de foie gras? And Colby, the man who started this all, had Kristen Valliere on his arm and a silly grin on his face.

Tears of joy misted Sunny's eyes. There he was—tall, handsome, and hers.

And those tears spilled over during the vows when he held Sunny's hand and proudly announced, "I'm yours forever."

Port Serenity Series

A Texas State of Mind
Texas Born
Texas Road Trip
Texas Double Date

Available on

www.bellastoriapress.com
Amazon
Barnes and Noble Nook
Kobo
iTunes

Ann DeFee is an award-winning author of eleven novels and one novella under various Harlequin imprints. Her debut book, A Texas State of Mind (2005) was a double finalist in the national Romance Writers of America's prestigious RITA contest and a Romantic Times nominee for Best First Series Book. In addition, Summer After Summer (2007) won the national Book Buyers' Best Long Contemporary award. Her current business venture is Bellastoria Press, a small publishing company that acquires and distributes books in both digital and print format. Her latest stories are in the Magical Realism genre including— Believe and Lucy's Got a Lot of 'Splaining to Do.

Please join her online at:
www.ann-defee.com
Facebook – anndefeeauthor
Ann DeFee, P.O. Box 266, Lightfoot, VA 23090

Ann's Booklist

A Texas State of Mind—Bellastoria Press LLP
Texas Born—Bellastoria Press LLP
Texas Road Trip—Bellastoria Press LLP
Texas Double Date—Bellastoria Press LLP
Goin' Down To Georgia—Harlequin American
The Man She Married—Harlequin American
The Perfect Tree—Harlequin American
Top Gun Dad—Harlequin American
Hill Country Hero—Harlequin American
Summer After Summer—Harlequin Everlasting
Beyond Texas—Harlequin Carina Press
A Hot Time In Texas—Harlequin Carina Press
Lucy's Got a Lot of 'Splaining to Do—
Bellastoria Press

Annaliese Darr

Believe—Bellastoria Press LLP

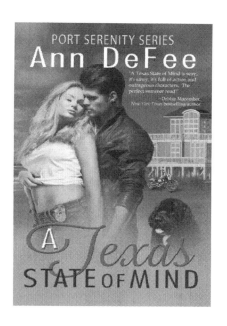

A Texas State of Mind

Book #1 of the Port Serenity
Series

Excerpt

Sage green eyes. Long, long lashes. Sensual lips. Every woman's fantasy. Bradley Cooper was going in for a world-class lip lock—and then Police Chief Lolly LaTullipe's phone rang, destroying her Netflix fantasy.

Lolly had never had a kiss that hot. Wendell, her ex, wasn't exactly a Romeo, and after he hightailed it out to Las Vegas to find fame and fortune as a drummer, her kissing had been limited to her kids and the dog.

Good old Wendell—more frog than prince. But to give credit where credit was due, he'd managed to sire two of the most fantastic kids in the world.

Nowadays she didn't have to worry about Wendell's flagging ego, or for that matter, any of his other wilting body parts. Celibacy had some rewards. Not many, but a few.

The phone rang again. "Great, just great," Lolly muttered as she turned off the DVR.

"Chief, I hate to call you at night, but I figured you'd want to handle this one. I just got a call from Bud out at the Peaceful Cove Inn, and he's got hisself something of a problem." An eight o'clock call from the Port Serenity Police Department's gravel-voiced night dispatcher signaled the end to her evening of popcorn and chick flicks.

Her hectic life as a single mom and head of a small police force left her very little free time, and when she had a few moments she wanted to spend them at home with Amanda and Bren, not out corralling scumbags.

"Cletus is on duty tonight, and that man can handle anything short of a full scale riot," Lolly argued, even though she knew her objections were futile.

Lordy. She'd rather eat Aunt Sissy's fruitcake than abandon the comfort of her living room, especially when Bradley was showing off his talents. Lolly hadn't even been able to find Mr. Sorta Right, although she'd given it the old college try. Wendell looked pretty good on the outside, but inside he was like an overripe watermelon–mushy and tasteless. Too bad she hadn't noticed that shortcoming when they started dating in high school. Back then his antics were cute; at thirty-seven they weren't quite so appealing. Good thing he'd been gone for almost eight years.

"I'd really rather not go out tonight."

"Yes, ma'am. I understand. But this one involves Precious." The dispatcher chuckled when Lolly groaned.

Precious was anything but precious. She was the seventeen- year-old demon daughter of Mayor Lance Barton, Lolly's boss and a total klutz in the single-dad department. She and Lance had been buddies since kindergarten, so without a doubt she'd be making an unwanted trip to the Peaceful Cove Inn.

"Oh, man. What did I do to deserve that brat in my life?" Lolly rubbed her forehead in a vain attempt to ward off the headache she knew was coming. "Okay, what's she done now?"

"Seems she's out there with some guys Bud don't know, and she's got a snoot full. He figured we'd want to get her home before someone saw her."

Lolly resisted a sigh. "All right, I'll run out and

see what I can do. Call her daddy and tell him what's happening."

She muttered an expletive as she marched to the roll-top desk in the kitchen to retrieve her bag, almost tripping over Harvey, the family's gigantic mutt. She strapped on an ankle holster and then checked her Taser and handcuffs, a girl had to be prepared.

Amanda, her ten-year-old daughter was immersed in homework, and as usual, her fourteen-year-old son had his head inside the refrigerator.

"Bren, get Amanda to help you with the kitchen." Lolly stopped him as he tried to sneak out of the room and motioned at the open dishwasher and pile of dishes in the sink. "I've got to go out for a few minutes. If you need anything call your Mee Maw."

Her first-born rolled his eyes. "Aw, Mom."

Lolly suppressed the urge to laugh, and instead employed the dreaded raised eyebrow. The kid was in dire need of a positive male role model. Someone stable, upright, respectable, and…safe. Yeah, safe. It was time to find a reliable, dependable prince—an orthodontist might be nice, considering Amanda's overbite.

"I'm leaving. You guys be good," Lolly called out as she opened the screen door.

A kaleidoscope of color from the garish neon beer signs reflected off puddles in the pitted asphalt. What a dump! Lolly parked her police SUV and checked out the current clientele of Port Serenity's most infamous dive. A couple of Bubba pickups, a red Mustang convertible and a shiny chrome Harley—nothing that sent up immediate red flags. Nevertheless, she patted her purse, ready for any situation.

Describing the Peaceful Cove as an inn was akin to calling a whorehouse a ladies' knitting club. With its peeling paint and plastic sign hanging at half-mast, it was, in fact, a hole-in-the wall eyesore, and redneck central for Lolly's little part of the Texas Gulf Coast. For years, Port Serenity's city fathers had been trying to get rid of the place. A category-four hurricane would probably be the only thing that would actually do the trick.

When Lolly stepped inside, she was almost bowled over by the noxious odor of stale beer, cigarette smoke and sweat. As she did a quick reconnaissance of the room, she noticed a man and woman engrossed in a pool game and two men sitting at a table in the shadows. A hoot of laughter came from a booth in the corner where Precious and her friends were holding court.

Lolly glanced at the problem kids before she strolled over to the bar to talk to a grizzled old man halfheartedly wiping the wooden surface. "Hey Bud, I heard you called." She avoided looking at the filthy rag in his hand. Her gag reflex was alive and well, thank you. "They been giving you a hard time, or are you just trying to keep from having trouble?" Lolly nodded over her shoulder.

"Don't want the Mayor on my butt. I wouldn't serve 'em nothing, cause if those girls ain't underage, my old coon dog's a squirrel. Then them boys got lippy. The only reason they backed off was that mean looking son-of-a-gun in the black T-shirt told 'em to sit down and shut up. Guess they didn't want to take him on." Bud chuckled. "Even those sissy college boys ain't that stupid."

Ann DeFee

Lolly studied the man in question. Bud had nailed him to a T. With the physique of a pro linebacker and a slicked-back ponytail the color of midnight, he was a poster child for America's Most Wanted.

Nope–this one wasn't a choirboy, and he was watching her like a mountain lion eying his prey. Ooh, yeah, she'd have big trouble on her hands if he realized she was a police officer. So she'd make sure he didn't.

"Pour me five Cokes, and I'll get rid of the brats for you." Lolly winked at Bud and took another peek at the man in the shadows.

Christian Delacroix was bored. He was fed up with his life, his job as an undercover cop for the Texas Department of Public Safety, Narcotics Division, and with swilling warm beer waiting for a sleazy informant to show up. As far as he was concerned the Houston drug dealers could kill each other off, and he'd stand back and applaud. Unfortunately, this backwater town was the key to his current investigation.

Another burst of laughter distracted him. What he wouldn't give to teach those frat boys a few manners. But if he acted on that impulse, he'd be up to his ass in paperwork, and paperwork was the last thing he needed.

What he really wanted to do was settle down with a good woman. His current fantasy included a picket fence, a couple of kids and a golden retriever. Fat chance! Not with his job. But there was light at the end of the tunnel—the minute he finished this assignment, he was going to make some major changes, both professionally and personally.

So Christian brooded and watched the entrance

while C. J. Baker, his friend and fellow undercover narc, leaned his chair back on two legs and popped his gum in perfect rhythm to a Luke Bryan tune. Snap, crackle, pop. Snap, snap, crackle, pop, pop. Christian gritted his teeth on the last series of pops.

"Man, oh man, would you look at that," Christian muttered as he eyed a voluptuous blond Amazon in the doorway. Curvy enough to fulfill any man's fantasy, her luscious hips were encased in a pair of skintight jeans. Christian blinked. She had to be a hallucination created by his sex-starved libido. Spit pooled in his mouth as erotic visions of all that creamy skin washed over him.

He resisted the urge to whack himself upside the head. He was looking for Marion the Librarian, not Marilyn Monroe. And this was Marilyn Monroe and Sofía Vergara all wrapped up in one mouthwatering package.

"Oh, man," Christian's heartfelt mumble prompted his companion to quit popping his gum. Those jeans and that sexy saunter should be illegal, or at the very least stamped with a hazardous to your health disclaimer.

"Boy, she looks familiar." C. J. rubbed the back of his neck. "I'm sure I know her from somewhere."

"In your dreams, kid."

"No, I know her. Just give me a few minutes and I'll remember." C.J. slammed all four legs of the chair on the floor and stared.

"Don't strain yourself, kid. It'll give you hemorrhoids." Christian couldn't take his eyes off the blond, even though in his business a distraction could be

Ann DeFee

deadly.

C.J. tapped his fingers on his forehead. "It's coming, it's coming."

"Yeah, sure," Christian said, but all his attention was centered on Blondie at the bar. After a short conversation she hefted a tray of drinks and strolled toward the raucous kids.

"Why do you think she's still toting that purse?" C.J. asked. "It's as big as a suitcase."

Christian was wondering the same thing. "She's probably afraid the old geezer will steal her wallet." He chuckled when she plopped the tray on the kids' table with a crash.

"Oh, my God! I can't believe it." C.J. yelped. "That's Lolly Hamilton! She sure didn't look like that when we were in high school. She was stick-skinny, all legs and elbows. And she had thick glasses, too."

"Well, she's not stick skinny now!" And that, Christian thought, was the understatement of the century.

The ringleader of the college crowd produced a cell phone and drew a nod of approval from Blondie. She listened to the phone conversation for a few minutes and apparently felt confident that the problem was solved because she turned and headed for the bar.

"She might not recognize me. We didn't exactly run in the same crowd," C.J. said. "Lolly was a bookworm and I was kind of wild."

"Oh really," Christian scoffed. "I have a hard time believing she was ever a wallflower. But you're still a wild man." He took a pull on his beer while he enjoyed her attributes—until she stopped dead in her

240

tracks, stared at C.J. and then broke into a million-dollar smile.

"Cookie Baker! Oh, my land. I can't believe it's you."

"Did she just call you Cookie Baker?" Christian's comment elicited a scowl from the blond beauty. Why was she glaring at him, and where was that wonderful smile?

"Last thing I heard, you were a Marine. Are you still in the military?" she asked C.J., deliberately ignoring Christian.

C.J. grinned and tipped his chair back. "Nope. I got out a while ago."

"Yeah, my friend here isn't exactly the military type." Christian felt compelled to join the conversation, even though he hadn't been invited. There was something about the woman that got under his skin.

Then she turned her back on him. Well, if that didn't fry him to a crisp. What had he done to warrant the cold shoulder? Nothing, absolutely nothing! Still, he couldn't believe what he was considering. It had to be the devil on his shoulder. That sucker always got him in a mess of trouble. But trouble or no trouble, he was about to teach this delectable morsel a lesson on hospitality, Texas style.

It was a huge mistake, he'd be the first to admit it, but he couldn't help himself. Without a word, Christian put his arm around her waist and jerked the blond bombshell into his lap.

Lordy mercy! Lolly couldn't believe she'd pulled such a brainless stunt. Even as a rookie she'd known better than to turn her back on a guy like him. Stupid! Stupid! Stupid!

Now she was plunked on his lap with his arms planting her firmly in place. Not only that, he had the nerve to be nuzzling the sensitive skin of her neck with his five-o'clock stubble. Sure, the guy was grade-A sex on the hoof—whew, she mentally fanned herself just thinking about it—but he probably had a rap sheet a mile long.

Lolly reached into her purse, flipped on her stun gun and silently counted to ten waiting for it to charge. She told herself that was the reason she let him snuggle those few extra moments. Then she pulled out of his grip and smiled. "Sugar, I think you need to learn some manners."

He fell like a giant redwood when she zapped his bare arm with the 65,000 volts.